DEVARIAN UPRISING
DEVARIAN CHRONICLES 2

BY

SIERRA DAFOE

Determined to secure the freedom of the pleasure slave she has come to love, Guardian Captain Soleyla Devarian makes a pact with Rolen, the leader of the Antoreans. She will turn traitor to her own people and help Rolen destroy the advance team sent to prepare his planet for colonization by the Nine-Star League. If they are successful, Rolen vows to put his people at her disposal in the final quest to gain Kantou's freedom — by overthrowing the very League itself!

But in her single-minded dedication to Rolen's cause, will Soleyla risk losing her beloved Kantou? And can Rolen bring himself to face the terrifying rigors of the one plan Soleyla can come up with to defeat the Guardians' superior forces?

WARNING: This book contains explicit sexuality, anal penetration, and voyeurism.

This book was previously published many years ago and has been reedited for its rerelease.

A Love Romances & More Staff Pick! "Ms Dafoe continues to impress with her ability to write scorching yet moving sexual encounters."

An ECataRomance Reviewer's Choice Nominee! "The reader will not be able to put this book down . . . The next book in this series promises to be a blockbuster!"

5 Blue Ribbons! "Breathtakingly erotic! Truly a sci-fi series that should not be missed." Romance Junkies

5 Flags! "Once again, Sierra Dafoe delivers steaming sensuality, and I believe surpasses her first entry in this powerful series. Readers, DO NOT MISS this book." Euro-Reviews

Devarian Uprising
Copyright © 2023 Sierra Dafoe
ISBN: 978-1-4874-3931-6
Cover art by Martine Jardin

Published by eXtasy Books Inc

Look for us online at:
www.eXtasybooks.com

CHAPTER ONE

Soleyla Devarian opened her eyes, feeling more at peace with herself than she had in months. A gray half-light filled Rolen's tent, trickling around the leather tent-flap and laying soft shadows across the rugs covering the earthen floor. She listened, letting her mind return slowly to alertness, enjoying the small noises of the cool predawn silence — the twitter of a bird, somewhere in the distance, and the gentle flapping of the hide tent under a brief, gusting breeze.

What a strange path had led her to this moment! It had begun, as so many things had for her, on Porto. Warm, exotic Porto, famous for its sparkling seas, its sandy beaches — and its pleasure slaves.

Intuition, if you will allow an old man his follies, tells me this one might be worth your consideration.

Merkun, the old trader who had sold her Kantou, had been hesitant, not wishing to offend, but he needn't have worried — his intuition had been right. Kantou stirred her as no man ever had.

Rolling to her right, she curled herself against Kantou, fitting her body tightly against his lithe, lean one. With a light touch, she traced the vicious, interlaced scars that crisscrossed his back. Her smile faded as her finger followed each hard raised weal, and Soleyla frowned, remembering old Merkun's words.

You are not your mother, my lady.

How had he known? Other than that one day, six years before, when Rachel Devarian had taken her inexperienced young daughter to Merkun's establishment to purchase her first pleasure slave, Danel, Soleyla had never met the man. Had Merkun, sensing the rage and rebellion in Soleyla after her mother had wrenched Danel from her, somehow known what would come of her relationship with Kantou?

Soleyla shook her head. Impossible. No one could have predicted the combination of events that had led her here, to Rolen's tent. But Merkun had certainly intended for her to discover who had left the scars on Kantou's back.

What had he thought she would do then?

Even in the midst of such ruminations, Soleyla stretched luxuriously, aware of her sense of utter relaxation. Last night's interlude, she knew, had had much to do with it, easing the sexual frustration that had seethed inside her for the past five weeks — weeks during which she had ruthlessly kept her desires in check, waiting for Kantou to learn to trust her.

The image of him as he'd been last night, standing before Rolen, claiming his right to *choose* to serve her, brought with it a rush of tenderness so deep it was almost painful. As he'd knelt before her, pliant and submissive, Soleyla had felt her breath catch in her throat. He was so beautiful!

A dozen recollections crowded back — Kantou's profile as he bent over the tracker he'd adjusted, increasing the instrument's range in the mountainous terrain of Antoros, his eyes, smoky with remembered pain as he'd asked if she would ever beat him. His face, softened by arousal, those full, curved lips damp with her juices as he lifted his head to gaze up at her . . .

Kantou. Her beautiful, lovely, precious Kantou. He was worth every risk she was about to take.

Softly, Soleyla traced a finger along one high cheekbone, outlined the taut muscles of his broad, angular shoulder, gathered the gleaming fall of his long, ash brown hair away from the nape of his neck, and kissed it.

He shifted slightly, sighing, and rolled onto his back.

Soleyla let her hand slide over the smooth expanse of his chest, down the slim, tapered plane of his abdomen to where his huge cock lay quiescent against his muscular thigh. Her mouth watered as she stroked it lightly, feeling Kantou respond even in his sleep to her touch. His cock stirred, lengthening beneath her fingers, and Soleyla felt a stab of heat between her thighs.

How she wanted that enormous cock inside her! But she could feel Rolen's bulk on the other side of the bed, sound asleep. Sighing, she dropped her hand away from Kantou's hardening shaft. When she finally took Kantou inside her, she wanted it to be private, just the two of them. A joining that no one — not even Rolen — would share.

Soleyla felt her smile returning. Rolen had been so contemptuous of Kantou. Mocking his submissiveness, unwilling — or unable — to admit that any man might be subservient to a woman by choice. Soleyla's lips curved in amusement at how quickly Rolen had changed *that* tune.

A second, more insistent throb of desire pulsed through her at the memory of the two men, one dark, one fair, fondling each other at her command, teasing themselves — and her — into a state where even the massive black-haired Antorean had ached to do her bidding.

And would do so again. In bed, and out of it.

Soleyla felt a most uncharacteristic desire to giggle.

The rage which had fueled her from the moment her mother had stripped her of Danel and exiled her to Antoros — a rage which had simmered, she realized suddenly, for years, was gone. It was only now, in its absence, that she could identify the deep, enduring emotion which had propelled her through six grueling years of Guardian training, determined to win a commission in their elite ranks and thus escape her mother's grasp. Or so she'd naïvely believed. But as a Guardian, she'd been more under her mother's control than ever.

Rachel Devarian, First Senator of the Nine-Star League and regent of the League's capital planet, Argulus, held the authority to command the Guardians when and where she would. And since the appearance of the bellicose V'ranyii, almost twenty years before, Rachel had ruled the Senate — and the League — with a cool, inflexible fist.

Not any longer.

Last night Soleyla had sworn a new vow. Rashly, no doubt, but it hardly mattered. Looking up at the hide ceiling of Rolen's tent, she admitted that the very act of declaring rebellion against her mother was in large part what had freed her from her silent, seething fury.

Instead, an unaccustomed giddiness race along her limbs. She, Soleyla Devarian, was going to overthrow the Nine-Star League.

Grinning, Soleyla slid from between the two sleeping men. Crossing to the table, she broke a hunk of sharp, pungent-smelling cheese from the wedge that lay there and washed it down with the remains of last night's wine as she glanced around the tent.

It was fairly spacious, containing a chest in addition to the table, hand-carved chairs, and the huge pile of furs that served Rolen as a bed. More comfortable than she would have expected for a rough emergency camp.

Idly, she picked up Rolen's sword. She swung it lightly, testing the heft of it — and then stopped, peering intently at the crossbar.

"There's just something about a naked woman with a sword in her hand."

Soleyla looked up. Rolen was watching her from the bed, one arm curled lazily behind his neck, his eyes, so deep a blue they were almost black, still heavy with sleep. The sight of his thick ebony hair, sticking out in odd directions, made her grin. "Oh, really?"

He sat up, revealing a body that was built on a Herculean

scale — broad, powerful shoulders, chest like an ox, with a heavy dusting of black curls tapering to a trail down the center of a stomach that rippled like waves of iron.

That wasn't the only thing like iron this morning, Soleyla noted.

Rolen nodded at the sword. "It was my father's. And my grandfather's."

"And your grandmother's before that."

"What?" Startled, Rolen rose.

Soleyla flipped the sword over and laid it on the table. "Look."

As he peered at the pommel, his forehead wrinkling in puzzlement, Soleyla laid her own sword beside it. "The lines have changed — the pommel's shorter, the balance higher — but this is a Guardian sword. Here." She turned her blade over as well, and Rolen's eyes widened. In the metal of both, just below the crossbar, was etched the same pattern, nine interlocking circles, and below it, a name. Bending close, Soleyla read the worn engraving. "Merrin Trafalgar. Captain. Antoros was settled by Guardians, Rolen."

"But . . . how? Why?"

For the same reason, Soleyla suspected that she herself was here. "There was a ship that disappeared, the *Star Strider*. Two centuries ago." Her gaze rested on Kantou as she spoke, drinking him in. He'd shifted as Rolen rose, and lay now with one arm thrown over his head, his long legs flung out. He looked so innocent, so vulnerable, sleeping with his head tilted back, exposing the strong, graceful curve of his neck. Soleyla felt a fierce stab of protectiveness.

Had Merrin Trafalgar once felt the same way? Soleyla rather suspected she had. "There was no distress signal, no emergency beacon. Nothing. The ship just disappeared." She looked at Rolen, her eyes bright. "I think Captain Merrin went renegade. She and all her crew."

"But . . ."

As she had, Rolen turned to study Kantou. She saw him frown slightly, perhaps remembering the unexpected ecstasy he'd discovered in another man's body. Perhaps thinking of the scars that laced Kantou's back.

Soleyla spoke softly. "Not all of us think men should be slaves, Rolen."

"I know."

Rolen's voice was equally quiet but roughened by complex emotions. It couldn't be easy, yet, for him to trust her. Not after what he'd seen Guardians do to his men. The League's advance team had been given explicit instructions for preparing Antoros for settlement—subdue the native population, and if they couldn't, exterminate them. Soleyla still shuddered at Rolen's tale of the three men who'd survived one of the earliest Guardian attacks, only to be raped by the entire advance team. No, Soleyla thought, it couldn't be easy at all.

"Rolen."

He looked at her, and from the haunted expression in his eyes, Soleyla knew she was right. He had agreed to help her, had pledged his life and his men to her cause in return for her help in rescuing Antoros from the League's encroach-ment—but his agreement had been born out of desperation, not trust.

There was only one argument she could make, one reassurance she could give him. Soleyla raised one hand and placed it gently on Rolen's chest. His skin was warm under her hand, smooth and taut over the hard, curved muscles. "Rolen, I swear to you, by my blood and my life, if there is any way to free your planet, we will do it."

For a moment, the emotion that blazed in Rolen's eyes reminded her sharply of Kantou. The pleasure slave had looked at her just like this, the day she'd bought him. Torn between hope and dread, wanting so badly to believe in her, and terrified of the depth of that want.

Soleyla could think of only one way to assuage that fear. Glancing at the bed, she was glad to see that Kantou was still asleep. Better that way. This was for him, for the sake of his freedom—but she didn't particularly want him to see what she was about to do.

Last night, Rolen had learned an appreciation of *her* sexuality, *her* desires, had submitted himself to her every wish and command. Now, the question was, did she have the courage to do the same?

Dropping her hand back to her side, Soleyla stammered, embarrassed, "I . . . Rolen, I don't know how to do this . . ."

"How to do what?"

"This." Naked, uncertain, she stepped into his arms, tilted her head back, and kissed him lightly.

The feel of his cool, firm lips brushing against her own sent a wholly unexpected quiver through her body. He cupped her chin gently in one hand, trailing the other one through her hair.

The sensation was utterly unlike anything she'd felt before. His touch was soft, reassuring, but at the same time determined, like a man soothing a restive horse he has every intention of riding. Something in her fluttered beneath his caress, like a startled bird wanting to fly—but her very nervousness made her acutely aware of the roughness of his fingertips, so different from Kantou's, moving delicately over her hypersensitive skin. She shivered, feeling goose bumps rise as Rolen's hand slid down her spine to the small of her back.

As he pulled her to him, Soleyla realized she was almost panting. Then he crushed his mouth down upon hers and she was aware of nothing but his tongue sliding between her lips, the rush of saliva in her mouth, the feel of her breasts pressed against his pecs. The tent spun, and a sudden burst of wetness slicked her passage.

Then he was lifting her, his biceps bulging as he clasped

her to him, scooping one arm under her ass to lower her to the floor. Soleyla found herself on her back, grateful for the rugs over the cool earth, staring up at Rolen who bent over her, his erection twitching slightly with each pulse of his heart. It was not so large as Kantou's, nor as long, but the head was full and firm, brushing against his hard stomach as he looked down at her, his gaze moving over her body with an intensity that made her breath go short.

"Rolen . . ."

"Shh." Shifting so that he was kneeling between her thighs, he reached out, following with his hands the trail his eyes had marked from shoulder to breast, caressing theirlush, heavy curves, then sliding his hands down her lithe sides, all the while watching, watching . . .

Soleyla lay under his gaze, feeling exposed in a way she never had before. She was not entirely sure she liked it. It was unnerving being scrutinized so slowly, so thoroughly.

For the first time in her life, Soleyla Devarian, Guardian captain and daughter of a planetary regent, found herself wondering what a man thought of her.

Rolen's eyes glittered, and his cock was rigid with desire. The urge to take him, right then, to shove him onto his back and mount him, riding him till the gnawing hunger inside her was assuaged, was hard to resist, but she did. This was not about pleasure, not hers anyway.

Even as they had used and broken his men, the Guardians had also taken something from Rolen—taken it without ever having touched him. With no more than a dim under-standing of what that something was, Soleyla knew there was only one way to repair the damage that had been done. She lay still, letting him touch her, study her as he liked.

His hands slid down, tracing the curve of her ass. Then he spread her legs, pressing her thighs back and apart. Soleyla braced herself, but he made no move to enter her. Instead, he stared down, rapt, at her sex, his gaze probing the damp, furred entrance spread wide before him. His tongue flicked between his teeth briefly, moistening his lips. His cock, a hard, erect pillar jutting up from between his thick powerful thighs, throbbed.

Pinioned beneath his stare, Soleyla shuddered, uneasy and aroused. He was massive, a full foot taller than she. And stronger, Soleyla admitted. Weaponless, she'd have little chance against the huge Antorean. And yet, as his gaze rose again to her face, studying it with a strange, yearning intensity, Soleyla felt, not dread, but a foreign sense of power.

Suddenly she remembered the fond amusement that had danced in Maris's voice. Maris, the woman who had fed her while she was bound, captive, in a nearby tent.

Rolen? It'd take more than I'm up for to be his woman. I'm Jerril's.

How strange that had sounded to her, Soleyla, daughter of the League that she was! To speak so casually of belonging to a man . . . and yet, as she lay beneath him, quivering in anticipation of his touch, it occurred to Soleyla to wonder what it might be like to belong to such a man.

She arched her back, and saw Rolen's gaze move back to her full, round breasts, her nipples dark and taut with arousal. That odd sense of power redoubled as she saw his pupils dilate, transfixed by the sight of her twin mounds.

Was this what Kantou felt when he knelt before her? Pliant, yielding, utterly submissive to her will, did he yet feel this strange rush, this compelling knowledge of his own desirability? Did he know what he *did* to her, every time she looked at him?

He must. Surely he must know by now how she felt about him.

Still, she was glad he was asleep. Soleyla glanced again at the bed. Kantou hadn't so much as moved.

Rolen, however, had. Bracing himself on his arms, he

lowered himself over her, nuzzling her neck as his cock nudged insistently at her opening. Smiling, Soleyla shifted her hips, and felt him slide into her.

"Oh, Soleyla," he breathed, his breath warm against her ear. His shaft felt like liquid iron inside her, hard and yet fluid, slipping easily into her depths. She lifted herself to meet him, and felt him tense, already on the edge. Lifting his head, he grinned down at her.

"Not so fast, woman. I've a mind to ride you all morning." His eyes sparked with merriment, like sunlight dancing on a deep ocean. "I like you in this mood."

A flicker of annoyance tensed her jaw for a moment. Consciously, she relaxed it, forcing herself to remember why she was doing this. Then she gasped as Rolen grabbed her arms, dragging them above her head and pinioning them with his hands about her wrists.

She struggled, aware even as she did that each movement, every tensing of her muscles, only increased the pressure on Rolen's cock inside her. His eyes darkened in pleasure, and she could feel his balls against the lips of her sex, hard and tight. Abruptly, she ceased struggling, and looked up at him soberly.

"Tell me something, Rolen. If I asked you to release me right now, would you?"

"Do you want me to?" His eyes were equally sober, now, but still dark with desire. A half-smile quirked at his lips as he waited for her answer. And waited. And waited.

His smile widened, and carefully wrapping one hand around both her wrists, he lowered the other to her breast, cupping it lightly as he flicked the nipple with his strong, rough fingers. "I didn't think so."

Soleyla bit her lip, furious with herself, then felt a jolt of fire shoot through her as Rolen tweaked her nipple, hard. "Tell me to release you, then."

His face, just inches from her own. His eyes, probing, insistent, as he rocked his hips, slicking his cock back and forth through her free-flowing juices.

"Tell me."

Obstinately, Soleyla gritted her jaw. She wouldn't give him the satisfaction. Rolen pulled himself back, sliding his cock almost fully out of her, then thrust it, hard and deep, into her throbbing passage. Furious, Soleyla heard herself moaning in pleasure, and he withdrew again only to slam himself home once more.

"Tell me, Guardian bitch."

At that, she looked directly at him. "No."

Grinning, he pulled out of her and with a strength that left her breathless, flipped her onto her belly. Soleyla scrambled to her knees, and immediately recognized her mistake as Rolen grabbed her, one hand on her hips, one closing in her hair, pinning her as he entered her from behind. He forced her head down until she was lying, ass tilted high in the air. Soleyla felt him swell inside her, aroused further by her struggles.

So, she realized, was she. Rolen's cock dragged against her swollen lips, teasing them as he pistoned in and out of her, his pace slowly increasing. His thrusts caused her breasts to drag back and forth against the rough weave of the rug, teasing her nipples into points of fire. Need surged through her, a desire she'd never before felt. He was fucking her like she was a dog, like she was a pleasure slave, and yet she *wanted* this man to ride her, to take his pleasure out on her.

Shocked, Soleyla repeated the admission to herself. Yes. She wanted that.

Snaking one hand down between her thighs, she ran her fingers over Rolen's balls, prodding them, feeling their taut fullness, and heard Rolen's breath roughen. Releasing her hair, he slid both hands to her ass, grabbing her cheeks and

11

spreading them wide. Soleyla closed her eyes as she imagined what the sight must be doing to him, looking down to watch himself plunge into her. His grip tightened, pinching her flesh, but even that added to her pleasure, betraying as it did how aroused he was, how close to losing control.

Experimentally, she pressed back against his hard thrusts and heard him groan as her muscles clamped down around him. Utterly inexperienced in the arts, in the very *idea* of trying to please a man, Soleyla smiled at the success of her maneuver. Levering herself up on one strong arm, she released his balls and slid her finger through her own springy curls, pressing her clit even as she caressed the sides of Rolen's shaft. The double stimulation of his cock filling her and her own fingers rubbing her clit made Soleyla moan like a wild thing.

The sound pushed him to the brink, and Soleyla gasped as Rolen, grabbing her hips, pulled her back against him, thrusting his cock into her so hard she felt his balls smashing against her working fingers. Soleyla rubbed her clit harder, faster, feeling the heat inside her flare up, feeling Rolen ram himself into that heat with an abandon that only fed her need.

Shoving her forward so that her breasts and cheekbone were pressed against the floor, he yanked her legs further apart, spreading her wide. Impatiently, he drove himself deep into her, and Soleyla felt the first, driving spurt of his orgasm. Her thighs trembled beneath Rolen's weight. Something black and greedy roared within her, and Soleyla shoved back against him as her fingers pressed hard against her throbbing clit and pushed her, shuddering with ecstasy, over the edge.

Her muscles clamped down around his shaft, drawing a fresh burst of hot, salty fluid from him. She heard him groan with pleasure as his balls spasmed, and his body, taut as a drawn bow, quivered with the force of his release.

For a moment they stayed rigid, their bodies shuddering

with reaction. Then Rolen slumped above her, his chest resting on her back. He shook as if with cold. But as he slid out of her and rolled to one side, drawing her down with him so that she lay on her back, her head pillowed on the rolling muscles of his shoulder, Soleyla realized that Rolen was laughing.

His eyes twinkled as she looked up at him, and he grinned. "Now you know how I felt last night."

Soleyla chuckled. "Then I think you owe me a thank you."

His expression grew serious, intent. "Thank you."

He wasn't talking about the sex.

She nodded back, equally serious. "We *will* do this, Rolen. If it can be done, we will do it."

The look in his eyes deepened, letting her see again a brief glimpse of his emotions—his agony, watching his people die, his terror that he wouldn't be able to save them, his hope, desperate and yearning, that Soleyla might somehow be their salvation. But this time she wasn't shut out of those emotions, cut off from them. This time, he let her in. With a sigh that was a half-sob, he crushed her to him, hugging her close with need and gratitude—and trust.

Soleyla closed her eyes, feeling a wholly unexpected bonding with this man, a leader struggling to protect his people. Different as he was, she could not help but respect him. He was courageous, dedicated, broad-minded enough to try allying even with her, a member of the enemy, if it might save his planet . . .

Opening her eyes, Soleyla grinned at the massive Antorean. It was right. It was impossibly, unutterably *right* that he, the descendant of a renegade Guardian, should be the key to Kantou's freedom.

When he grinned back, Soleyla's rash vow suddenly didn't seem so insanely impossible to her. With an entire planet's population for an army, and Antoros as her base of operations . . .

13

Her head already buzzing with plans and possibilities, Soleyla gave Rolen one last squeeze and rose, dressing quickly. As she buckled on her sword belt, she glanced at the bed where Kantou, still asleep, had curled onto his side, his face half- hidden by his arm.

Whatever it cost, whatever it took, she *would* set him free.

Determined but hopeful, Soleyla flung open the tent-flap and stepped out into the clear morning air, whistling.

And stopped.

As Soleyla stared, aghast, at the sprawling camp, silent and drowsy in the clear morning air, the whistle died on her lips.

Knocked unconscious by two of Rolen's men, she had been dragged, bound and insensate, to the tent where she'd eventually awoken. By the time she'd freed herself from her bonds and escaped the tent, it had been too dark to make out much of her surroundings.

She'd assumed the camp was temporary, a makeshift outpost well away from the bulk of the Antorean population. But as she noted the milch animals grazing sleepily between the large, sturdy tents, the small patches of tended vegetables, the sleepy toddler who stumbled out of a nearby shelter to gaze blankly at her as he pissed before disappearing back inside, a terrible suspicion crept like ice into her gut.

This was her rebel force, her planetary army with which to conquer a galaxy?

There were three hundred tents, perhaps, scattered across the broad northern plain.

Rolen came to stand beside her, his eyes gleaming with a fierce, protective love as he gazed out over the camp. Seeing his expression, Soleyla's suspicion turned to hideous certainty.

The sun was just creeping past the surrounding ring of mountains, spreading waves of tangerine and gold over the lush, dew-specked grass, the sleepy animals and the tents scattered over the northern plain. But to Soleyla, the world was suddenly as black as the darkness on the far side of a moon.

CHAPTER TWO

Crouched beside a fire, Kantou shivered. Above him, stars flickered in the velvety blackness of the vast Antorean sky.

For eight days he had watched Soleyla, her face set in a terrifying scowl, drill, train, and bludgeon the men of Rolen's tribe into some sort of fighting force by sheer force of will. That same intensity had carried over into the bed they shared with Rolen. The two men had found themselves lashed by her commands to almost frenzied peaks, writhing in ecstasy under her steely gaze.

She was a whirlwind, tireless, driven by some inner necessity beyond Kantou's understanding. He wondered sometimes, as she strode past him, unspeaking, whether she even remembered he was alive.

On the far side of the flames, a ragged, tow-headed boy squatted, studying him. Other fires flickered in the distance, dozens of them dotting the plain. Kantou huddled under the sheepskin cloak Maris had draped over his scarred shoulders and tried not to listen to the voices from the tent behind him — one deep and gruff, one higher and bell-like, both firm, impatient, used to command. The evening breeze veered, suddenly chilly, and carried fragments of their argument to Kantou's ears.

" . . . you mad? I *saw* what they did to—"

"If you can think of a better plan, I'd be happy to hear it." Soleyla's voice was like metal, sharp and deadly cold. Kantou shivered, and glanced up at the stars whose patterns were as

16

alien to him as the unknown creatures which had provided the mottled skins for the tents.

He didn't belong here. He didn't know where he belonged anymore.

From the tent, Rolen's voice rose in a bellow of fury. "You cannot ask this of me!"

On the other side of the fire, Betren, the tow-headed boy, shrugged his skinny shoulders eloquently. "My parents throw me out when they're arguing, too."

Kantou tried to muster an answering smile and failed. What did one say to a boy who, at eight years old, still ran to his mother for a quick, loving hug?

He had never known his mother. He wondered for the first time if she'd wanted, even briefly, to keep him. Or had she been eager to rid herself of a hated male child? To hand him over, as all male infants were, to the League's child-houses to be raised as a slave?

"If we can't get to those portals, Rolen, we're dead before we start." Soleyla's voice was hard, insistent. The iron inflexibility in her tone frightened Kantou.

Cocking his head to one side like an alert, curious bird, Betren asked, "Are you really from another planet?"

Kantou nodded briefly. It was all the response he could manage. A dull relief trickled through his distraction when Maris appeared, giving him an absent smile as she scolded her eldest son into their nearby tent.

The fire crackled and hissed. Above him, the stars spun slowly in their unfamiliar dance. People rose, yawning, from around the fires and disappeared, in ones and twos, into the scattered tents. Gradually the camp settled into silence. But the voices in the tent behind him continued, low and urgent, as the fire flared and guttered and slowly burned out.

Then the night was punctuated by Rolen's outraged shout. "I will not do it!"

Kantou heard the tent-flap flung open. Soleyla stormed past him, her back rigid with fury. She didn't even glance at him as she muttered, "Don't wait up," and stalked off into the darkness.

Hours later, long after the fire had died and even the coals gave off only fitful gleams, Kantou woke, feeling the growing cold gnaw into his bones. Soleyla still hadn't returned.

Why couldn't they be back in the mountains, just the two of them, planting relay transmitters for the communications grid? *Why* did they have to help these people? Why couldn't they just go back?

He didn't want to be here. He didn't even want the freedom she'd bestowed on him. He only wanted Soleyla.

She hardly spoke to him anymore, barely even acknowledged his presence.

Kantou glanced around the camp. At this late hour it seemed desolate, utterly empty of life. Even the herd beasts of the Antoreans slept in a silence that felt like death. The wind sighed and moaned, reaching wraithlike fingers under his cloak. Shivering, he rose and went into the only shelter he had.

A single candle flickered near the bed. By its light he saw Rolen, sprawled across the furs, naked and snoring. A wineskin slumped, three-quarters empty, on the table.

Quietly, Kantou shed his clothes and slid into the narrow space that was left, careful not to rouse the Antorean. The heat radiating off the sleeping man warmed him, and slowly Kantou's shudders eased.

His mind drifted, coming back, as it did over and over, to the image of Soleyla, stretched on the floor below Rolen, smiling up at him as he spread her legs wide. Like a man probing a sore tooth, Kantou flinched at the memory, but studied it, recalling every sigh, every moan as the two of them, believing him asleep, had coupled lustily on the floor.

Why wouldn't Soleyla let him inside her? The question haunted Kantou. He longed to penetrate that glorious, powerful body, feel her muscular thighs clamp around his waist, drawing him down into her. But each time he'd tried, she'd pushed him away.

Kantou's cock twitched as he imagined plunging into her, feeling her hot, slick passage around him, experiencing the ecstasy he'd seen on Rolen's face . . .

That was the thought which burned like acid. She'd allowed *Rolen* to fuck her.

Rolen, but not him.

Kantou rolled onto his side, hugging the furs close. A strange, clawing emotion for which he had no name shook his long, lean frame.

Maybe she doesn't want me anymore.

Once before, he'd let himself believe that. That night in the mountains when she'd turned away from him and strode into the darkness, he had been certain he'd lost her forever. She'd reassured him, and for a brief, shining moment Kantou had let himself believe she loved him. Soleyla Devarian, daughter of a League Senator, beautiful, brave . . .

How could she ever possibly love him? He was nothing, a pleasure slave.

No. He wasn't even that, now.

The realization was a knife, slashing into his very core. Heedless of the sleeping man next to him, Kantou moaned and curled into a ball, trying to push away the thought. But it only cut deeper, growing into a black, desolate certainty.

Soleyla had freed him, not because she loved him, but because she didn't want him anymore.

Tears coursed down his face as Kantou nodded to himself, the rough, hand-spun fabric of the sheet scraping against his cheek. It all made sense now. It fit. No wonder she pushed him away every time he tried to enter her. No wonder they never made love alone, without Rolen. Soleyla was tired of him.

And he no longer belonged to her.

His sobs became frantic. What was he, then, if not Soleyla's? He wanted nothing else. He knew nothing else. The future yawned before him, empty and terrifying, and he huddled beneath the scratchy wool blanket, hiding from it.

Never, not even as a toddler in the child-house on Marbul, had Kantou felt so utterly alone.

Roused by the sound of sobbing, Rolen swam dizzily out of a wine-fogged sleep. Raging, he'd paced and drunk himself into a stupor after Soleyla had stormed out, finally collapsing into inebriated unconsciousness. Now he lay for a moment, trying to imagine who could be crying in his bed.

For Rolen, the past week had been full of revelations. Soleyla defied every category of womanhood he'd ever encountered. Beautiful, ferocious, she was more woman than he'd ever seen — woman enough to master even him. The one time he'd mastered *her*, Rolen knew full well it was because she'd allowed it. She'd given him that. But in the nights that had followed, she'd demanded — and received — an absolute obedience that Rolen blushed to admit to. The experience was intoxicating, erotic in a way he could never have imagined. She used him, and Kantou, with a ruthlessness that made his head spin, flayed him to the core with the passions that buffeted his body.

Now, wakened by the sound of crying, he was amazed. It was almost impossible to picture the steely, self-assured Guardian captain reduced to tears. He reached out muzzily, and started as he found that the sobbing form he'd drawn into his arms wasn't Soleyla, but Kantou.

Rolen still hadn't come entirely to terms with the

enjoyment he'd found in another man's body, nor with Kantou's willing—hell, eager—submissiveness to Soleyla. It was all very well in bed. There was something uniquely arousing about obeying every desire she whispered in that stern, commanding voice, about being entwined between their two bodies. Sometimes he'd felt himself to be no more than a projection of Soleyla's will, a tool she used to fuck her Kantou—only no tool could take such delight in its employment. Even the sleep-fogged memory of their encounters sent a pulsing heat through Rolen's groin.

And now Kantou was lying in his arms, sobbing as if his heart would break. Nothing in his life had prepared Rolen for such a situation, any more than he'd been prepared for the intense attraction he felt toward the lithe, almost surreally beautiful pleasure slave. Inappropriate as it was, he found his cock growing hard as Kantou's body quivered against his own, reminding him sharply of Kantou's shudders of ecstasy when Rolen penetrated him at Soleyla's command.

Firmly, Rolen pushed that thought aside. Unsure what to do, he whispered, "It's all right, Kantou. Whatever it is, it's all right."

Kantou shook his head fiercely, and Rolen found himself instinctively drawing him closer, his hand rising to stroke Kantou's long, silky hair. Kantou lay with his head pillowed on Rolen's broad chest, shaking with the effort to control his sobs.

"Kantou, what is it?"

No reply. Helplessly, Rolen murmured meaningless words, trying to comfort him. The feel of Kantou's lean, muscular body pressed against him was almost painfully arousing. His cock hardened further, straining under the sheets. Furtively, he hoped Kantou wouldn't notice.

"Is there anything I can do?"

Kantou shook his head again. Then, almost noiselessly, he

21

whispered, "Make love to me."

Rolen froze, feeling a wave of pure lust flow through him. He was suddenly, acutely conscious of the emptiness of his large tent, the silence of the night around them. Kantou clung to him, unmoving, not even raising his head. There was such *need* in the younger man's voice, a need Rolen's cock was aching to fulfill.

But this wasn't like the times they'd caressed each other under Soleyla's watchful gaze. This was . . . different. Intimate in a way that was both frightening and irresistible. He could hear Kantou's breath, softer now but still ragged, and was uncomfortably aware of his own shallow breathing and the way every fiber of his body seemed to betray his arousal.

Slowly, Kantou lifted his head, his soft, heavy hair dragging across Rolen's skin. Rolen felt his nipples tighten in response. Then Kantou's mouth was moving gently over his chest, leaving a path of small kisses that burned like fire on his skin. When he reached Rolen's nipple, he flicked it with his tongue.

Rolen gasped, his head dropping back, his hand coming up automatically, closing in the younger man's hair as Kantou sucked his nipple between full, moist lips.

Rolen's cock throbbed in response, as if the band of muscle between his chest and groin was a direct conduit for the sensation.

Kantou released his nipple and slid lower, working slowly down to where Rolen's cock strained upward as if to greet him. He paused, snaking out his tongue to lick the very tip. Rolen jerked involuntarily, his hips rising off the bed, a first drop of fluid leaking from his slit. Delicately, like a cat, Kantou lapped it off, then swirled his tongue around the bulging head.

The stimulation was intoxicating. As Kantou took Rolen's cock in his mouth, flicking the underside of it with his tongue,

Rolen groaned. The urge to thrust upward, to fuck Kantou's mouth until he exploded inside it, was almost uncontrollable.

Gritting his teeth, he fought the hot, demanding hunger inside him. Then Kantou slid one hand around Rolen's balls, playing with their weight, and let his lips go soft and welcoming around Rolen's shaft.

With such an invitation, Rolen couldn't resist. Wrapping both hands in Kantou's thick, luxurious hair, he pistoned himself up into that warm, waiting mouth. Kantou moaned and plunged his head down, his lips stretching as he reached the very base of Rolen's shaft. Rolen felt the vibration of sound along the entire length of his cock. Clenching his jaw, he froze, fighting the sensations that surged through him. Kantou lapped his cock hungrily, catching his free-flowing come, working his fingers over and over Rolen's tight, swollen balls.

Rolen growled as he felt Kantou's throat tighten convulsively, swallowing his leaking juices. "Kantou, damn it, slow down."

Kantou drew back with obvious reluctance, his teeth trailing lightly over the veins of Rolen's cock. At the touch, Rolen felt his balls contract, and it took all his self-control not to come right then.

Gently, remembering the way the younger man had been crying, Rolen tugged Kantou upward. Reaching out a hand, he stroked Kantou's cheek, still damp with tears. Tilting Kantou's head up, Rolen looked into those luminous gray eyes, feeling a tenderness he'd never known for a man before. He drew Kantou down to him and kissed him, tasting his own slippery, salty tang on Kantou's lips.

With a deep, shuddering sigh, Kantou let his cheek rest on Rolen's broad shoulder. He turned his head, feeling Kantou's hair tickle his lips as he whispered, "I want to please you, Kantou. Will you let me do that?"

Kantou hesitated a moment, then nodded. Rolen felt the heat in his groin redouble as, with shaking hands, he drew Kantou upright, positioning the younger man above him. Running his hands up Kantou's long, lean thighs, Rolen cupped them around his warm, firm ass, drawing Kantou's cock to his lips.

Fully erect, it nudged against his waiting mouth. Once again, Rolen marveled at its size as he relaxed his jaw, allowing the huge tip to push slowly between his lips. The clean, musky scent of Kantou's balls filled his nostrils, making him snort like a horse and suck Kantou's velvety head deeper. He felt Kantou shudder, and with an inward smile grabbed his ass, spreading the cheeks wide.

Kantou gasped and arched his back, and Rolen obligingly slid a finger toward his asshole. It flexed and gaped under his probing touch, begging to be entered. He teased it, playing his fingers slowly around the rim while at the same time his mouth worked Kantou's cock. He felt Kantou relax into the dual stimulation. Slowly, the young man's hips started rocking back and forth, alternately driving his cock into Rolen's waiting mouth and shoving his hot, hungry ass back onto Rolen's probing finger.

Rolen could feel Kantou's balls dragging heavily against the hair on his chest, and suddenly sympathized with Kantou's impatience. He wanted Kantou to *fuck* him, damn it, wanted him to drill that gloriously huge cock deep into his throat, burning, punishing, until he drowned in Kantou's sweet juices.

But the pleasure slave had, he knew, more control than Rolen ever would. Keeping the same, even pace, Kantou slowly lengthened his strokes, sending his cock deep into Rolen's mouth, but never hard, never fast, never as wantonly as Rolen desired.

His own cock throbbed, and he could feel his hips flexing,

instinctively seeking a lover's touch. Ruthlessly, Rolen suppressed the motion. He'd taken pleasure from Kantou, over and over, and had worried very little about giving pleasure back. Now he was determined to make Kantou forget whatever had so badly grieved him—however he had to.

And, as he brought one hand up to wrap around the base of Kantou's impossibly thick, hard shaft, Rolen realized that, for once, Soleyla wasn't here to tell them what they could—or couldn't—do.

CHAPTER THREE

Soleyla strode through the night, feeling rage quiver along her spine. Did Rolen think they had endless alternatives, that he could afford to reject the one plan she'd managed to come up with which stood a chance of working?

Her first burst of panic as she'd discovered how small Rolen's numbers were had grown to dismay at their utter lack of martial training. Some four hundred men, farmers and herders utterly unused to fighting, against League-trained Guardians . . . It would be no battle, but a slaughter.

The ground grew rough under her feet as Soleyla worked her way deep into the steep foothills west of the camp, pounding her tension and anger out on the arid, shifting rocks. It was a path her feet were coming to know well.

What had she gotten herself into? A Guardian captain, sworn now to overthrow the League itself with a handful of barbarian tribesmen who could barely swing a sword!

Soleyla's lips twisted in the darkness, forming a self-mocking sneer. She was insane. It was impossible. She knew what the League Guardians were capable of, none better. She'd been one of them, trained alongside them . . .

Commanded them.

Swearing, Soleyla kicked a rock into the darkness, refusing to pursue that thought back into the bitter, poisonous dregs of memory. It was her command on Termigan IV that had cost her Danel.

Soleyla cursed roundly, damning Rolen, damning her mother, damning herself for having gotten into this mess. But she would *not* lose Kantou as she had Danel. If she had to fight, to kill, if she had to overthrow the very League itself to protect him, she would do it.

Such fine words! a voice inside her mocked. Soleyla flushed, recalling vividly how she'd stalked past Kantou earlier, seeing his great gray eyes darken with pain as she stormed past, barely deigning to acknowledge him.

How could she explain the fear that rode her, that would not allow her a moment's distraction as she drove Rolen's men, readying them for a battle they could never, ever win?

And the only plan she'd managed to devise, Rolen had refused. She understood his reluctance — none better — but without the one distraction she could think of, they stood no chance at all. Furious, she spat into the night, knowing that even her rage was only a mask for emotions she barely knew how to utter.

"Oh, Kantou," Soleyla whispered, her voice full of a yearning she couldn't allow herself to show — not now, not with so much riding on her. She completed the sentence only in her mind. *Would that we were a thousand light years from here, and alone.*

As she topped the first of the foothills, the vast ring of the northern mountains loomed above her, a shadowy bulk against the sky, blotting out the fading stars. If only she could do the same! Simply blot out the Nine-Star League, close herself off from it — herself and Kantou — into a small, warm space where not even Rachel Devarian's long arm could reach.

Thinking of Rolen's sword, and the long-dead Guardian who had wielded it, Soleyla felt a kinship with that unknown woman, Merrin Trafalgar. She'd give anything to be able to do what Merrin had done, just flee with her Kantou to someplace far beyond the League's control.

But where was there, now, to run?

Soleyla sank to the hillside, drawing her sword and laying

it across her knees. The waning night was cool, peaceful, soft with the moist spring breezes blowing up from the south. To Soleyla, that peace was deceptive. She could feel events building, massing on the horizon like a storm.

The ring of mountains swept away in a wide arc north, turning to plunge south again on the far side of the plain. Beyond them, the sky blushed with the first faint streaks of dawn. Soleyla studied them suspiciously through bloodshot eyes. What was happening beyond those craggy peaks?

By now, of course, Commander Valda could have 'ported in a whole battalion of Guardians, each trained as Soleyla herself was to a combat readiness these nomadic Antoreans couldn't even imagine. For all Soleyla knew, an entire army was lying hidden behind those mountains, readying itself to descend on the sleeping camp.

For all her apprehension, there was no doubt in Soleyla's mind about why she was doing this. The image of Kantou, waiting faithfully by the fire even as she stalked past him, was reason enough. She would not lose him. Kantou was *hers*. Hers alone. If she had to fight, to die, if she had to overthrow the League to gain his freedom, she would do it.

To fail was unthinkable. For herself it would mean execution as a traitor and a rebel—and Soleyla had no doubt that her mother would sign her death warrant without a single quiver in those cool, capable fingers. But for Kantou . . .

Soleyla shuddered, picturing the hideous, overlacing scars that marred the smooth skin of his back.

Oh, my beauty, what have I gotten us into?

Kantou felt as if he were being torn in two. His body writhed in erotic delight as he straddled Rolen, feeling the larger man's broad, muscled chest under his ass while Rolen's mouth and hands worked deliriously over his throbbing erection. His skin felt caressed by searing liquid fire, and he breathed in short, hard gasps to control the tension mounting in his balls.

But inside . . .

Kantou moaned and pushed his cock deeper into Rolen's waiting mouth, seeking oblivion in that hot, wet embrace. He could feel Rolen's tongue dancing over the shaft, urging him on, while his sphincter was penetrated by the Antorean's thick, heavy finger. He arched back to meet it, feeling it slide into him roughly — but not roughly enough to blot out the despair blackening his soul.

Soleyla didn't want him. Didn't need him.

Didn't love him.

Kantou dropped his head back, feeling his thick, heavy hair slide silkily over his back. Trapped between his internal agony and the ecstasy Rolen's mouth created, he writhed, his chest burning with pain, his cock with pleasure. In the space between was a hollow, gaping emptiness that threatened to swallow him whole.

He thrust his hips forward, feeling Rolen struggle to encompass the whole of his shaft. Rolen's eyes — a blue so deep they were almost black — gazed up at him hungrily. Yes, Kantou thought, Rolen wanted that. Wanted Kantou to fuck him, *hard*, fill him until he burst.

And why not? What was there left to lose? Soleyla had set him free. Why should he not use that freedom as he liked?

He leaned forward, bracing himself on his arms, and looked down, watching, as he pumped his shaft deep in Rolen's mouth. "You like that, don't you?"

Gagged by Kantou's cock, eyes half closed in ecstasy, Rolen nodded. The sudden pressure the motion created sent a jolt up Kantou's spine.

"Do you want more, Rolen?"

The gleam in Rolen's eyes was answer enough. Closing his own eyes, Kantou shoved the darkness inside him away and forced himself to feel nothing, nothing but the heat of Rolen's mouth, the full, firm lips tugging at his massive, swollen cock, sucking it deep, his tongue lashing like a snake over, around and under it.

Blindly, Kantou reached out, closing his fists in Rolen's thick, jet-black hair. Pinning Rolen in his grasp, he drove his shaft deep, plunging it into Rolen's mouth. Rolen's hand came up, grabbing Kantou's ass, urging him on as he sped up, pulling his cock out until Rolen's lips stretched around his hard, shiny tip, then thrusting, hard, as Rolen's fingernails raked across his ass cheeks, down his thighs. Rolen's eyes were closed in delirious hunger and suddenly Kantou *hated* him, hated him with a passion as hot and explosive as the pressure building up in his balls.

This man had fucked Soleyla. He had filled her hot, tight pussy with his cock, had groaned as he released his come into her. He had been allowed that — and Kantou loathed him for it.

Jerking his cock out of Rolen's mouth, he stared down at the Antorean. "No. No, you'd like that too much, wouldn't you?"

Rolen gazed back at him, his eyes confused. A hard grin knotted Kantou's cheeks. His balls were so full, they ached. Kantou squeezed them lightly, redoubling the pain. He remembered how Soleyla had commanded him to do just that, leaning forward, her lips slightly parted, her face flushed with arousal as she watched him.

The recollection raised an animalistic fury inside him. He wanted to *fuck*, damn it. Wanted to take his anguish and pain and thwarted desire out on this man who lay beneath him, flushed with arousal. This man who had come between him and his Soleyla.

Kantou growled through clenched teeth, "You really want to please me, Rolen?" He saw Rolen's eyes widen at the menace in his tone, but the Antorean nodded.

There was one thing Soleyla had not allowed them. They had masturbated each other, playing their fingers over each other's erect cocks, squeezing and tormenting each other's balls under her glittering gaze. They'd sucked each other off, their hips rocking in unison as they suckled and lapped, spilt their seed in each other's mouths. And Rolen had fucked *him*, oh yes, had buried his thick hard cock deep inside Kantou's ass.

But Kantou hadn't fucked Rolen.

"Turn over," he ordered. Rolen froze for a moment, staring at the club-like shaft of the younger man's cock. Kantou reached out and twisted his nipple cruelly. As Rolen gasped, his cock twitching with desire, Kantou grinned again.

"You want it rough, Rolen? You want me to fuck you, hard? Bury myself in that hot, horny ass?" As he spoke, he watched Rolen's face flush with shame and excitement. "You do, don't you?"

"Yes." The word was a whisper, breathed unwillingly into the shadows of the tent.

"Then turn over!"

Scrambling to his knees, Rolen turned around and bent over, thrusting his strong, muscular ass high in the air. Kantou fought back the surge that swelled through him, a deep, primal craving to shove himself home, pinion Rolen below him and thrust and thrust until his need was assuaged.

Reaching for the oil jar Soleyla had placed near the bed, Kantou slowly lubricated Rolen's ass. Probing with one finger, he shivered in anticipation. Gods! Rolen was so tight. Never having been violated by anything thicker than a wax candle, his asshole gripped Kantou's finger like a vise.

Kantou slid his finger back and forth, reaching around with his other hand to smear oil across the Antorean's thick cock. Rolen moaned under him, pushing his hips back as Kantou

pumped his fist up and down his shaft. Under the dual stimulation, Rolen's asshole relaxed, and he gasped as Kantou
worked a second finger into him.

"You like that, Rolen?"

Rolen moaned, tossing his head, and Kantou felt a bolt of
rage sear through him. Bastard! He took, and took, and found
nothing but pleasure in breaking Kantou's heart.

Now he would know what it was like to be the one taken.

Letting go of Rolen's cock, Kantou whipped his hand
around and brought it smacking squarely down on Rolen's
ass. "Answer me!"

Rolen jerked at the smack, his back stiffening. Kantou felt
Rolen's sphincter spasm around his fingers, clamping down.
Then the man below him rocked back, thrusting himself onto
the fingers invading him, and his breathing grew ragged as
his asshole relaxed further, almost begging to be violated. The
mark of Kantou's slap showed clearly on his white skin. Kantou looked at it and swallowed.

"Yes. Yes, I like it. I love it. Please . . ."

Kantou wouldn't have believed he could get any harder.
He was wrong. As Rolen squirmed under him heedlessly,
begging to be taken, he felt his cock swell further, jutting
spear-like at the hole into which his fingers now plunged.
Rolen's voice, harsh and urgent, rough with need, seemed to
vibrate in the pit of his stomach, sending shockwaves into his
engorged balls.

"Please, Kantou. I want you to fuck me. I want you to bury
your cock inside me. I want you to pound my ass. Please. Fuck
me, Kantou."

Writhing below him, Rolen wantonly rolled his hips, and
Kantou could wait no longer. Spreading Rolen's cheeks with
both hands, he placed the engorged purple tip of his cock
against that hot, pulsing opening. Rolen fell still beneath him,
his body relaxed, waiting.

Kantou's cock nudged against the tight, oiled rim, prodding. He could feel Rolen's concentration as the Antorean struggled to open himself as wide as he could, easing Kantou's entry. Rolen's hands came up and grabbed his own asscheeks, stretching them apart, and Kantou could see his balls, round and taut, just below that deliciously tight opening. Reaching down with one hand, he stroked them, and with the other guided his huge, throbbing shaft to Rolen's sphincter.

As he pressed, firmly and steadily, he felt the hard ring of muscle stretch to encompass his swollen head. It spasmed, almost sending him over the edge, and he stopped, rocking gently back and forth until the spasm eased. Rolen mewled like a cat below him, frozen in an ecstasy that Kantou knew was half agony, half stark lust. Then, as his body relaxed, adjusting to the gargantuan cock invading it, Rolen pushed back against him, allowing his cock to slide in deeper in deeper.

He was so hot inside! It was like entering a furnace. Rolen's asshole squeezed his swollen head so tightly it was almost painful. The pressure in his balls redoubled, urging him to piston forward, bury himself in that spread, waiting ass.

Kantou slid his hands to Rolen's hips and held himself there, arms quivering, his weight resting fully on the man beneath him, fire blazing along his every nerve. He felt his cock pulsating, spurting the first of its juices inside Rolen's ass. The added lubrication made it easy to push just a little bit farther . . .

The thick, meaty tip of his cock popped past the resistance and Kantou threw his head back, the cords of his neck standing out as Rolen's opening clamped down around the full width of his shaft. Kantou roared, his abs quivering with the strain of holding himself back, while below him Rolen gasped and stiffened. Tongues of flame shot through Kantou's balls, and he could feel his leaking cum slicking the hot sides of Rolen's passage. His breath hissed between his teeth as he dug his fingers into Rolen's hips and struggled for the control that had been drilled into him.

Why? Why was he holding himself back? The question was like a slap. Kantou's jaw gritted, and tears started to his eyes, heavy and stinging. He wasn't a pleasure slave any longer. He wasn't Soleyla's. He was nobody's. What reason, then, to be so considerate of this man below him, this man he had every reason to hate?

Loathing Rolen, despising himself, Kantou slammed his hips forward, burying his cock deep in Rolen's ass in one hard, punishing thrust. Lights burst behind his eyes. His head swam. For a moment he thought he might black out.

Then he heard Rolen whimpering in pain below him. Immediately, all his rage at the black-haired Antorean flickered like a candle and died, leaving only an ashen self-disgust. Pulling out as gently as he could, Kantou rolled onto his side, curling around the throbbing fire in his loins, his overloaded nerves sending streaks of fire through his shuddering body.

In the silence, he heard the blankets rustle as Rolen moved. Kantou waited, panting as he fought to contain the raging emotions that tore at him—shame, lust, and a longing for Soleyla so deep he knew it would haunt him forever. If Rolen swept up his sword and put an end to his miserable life right now, Kantou would do nothing but thank him as the blade pierced his unprotected back.

Instead, he felt a feather-light touch tracing the knotted lines of his scars. He gasped and tried to jerk away, but a warm, strong hand closed on his shoulder, holding him still as Rolen caressed his disfigured back.

"Who did this to you?" Rolen's voice was no more than a whisper.

Kantou shook his head, too dazed to reply. Firmly, Rolen pulled on his shoulder, rolling him back to face the Antorean. Kantou closed his eyes, unable to meet Rolen's gaze.

A breath stirred his hair, and he felt Rolen's cheek against his own, then a light kiss at the base of his earlobe.

"I wanted it, you know," Rolen said. Kantou opened his eyes to see Rolen looking down at him, his dark eyes wide and wondering. "I did. It was just too fast." Holding his gaze, Rolen lay back, one hand softly stroking Kantou's face.

How could he do that? Kantou stared in amazement. After what he'd just done . . .

As if reading his thoughts, Rolen grinned. "I *did* want it, Kantou." His grin faded, and his eyes shone with dark hunger. "I still do. I want you to fuck me, Kantou."

At his words, the floodgates inside Kantou burst open. Tears streamed from his eyes as he rolled to Rolen and kissed him. Rolen's lips parted, and his tongue slipped inside Kantou's mouth. Holding Rolen's face between his hands, Kantou responded in kind, their tongues entwining in an intimate dance even as Kantou sobbed.

He was barely aware of Rolen's hands on his body pulling him on top, of Rolen's thighs wrapping around his waist. One firm, strong hand closed around his throbbing cock and guided it back to Rolen's slick, tight hole. With blind, grieving need, Kantou pressed gently against it, and gasped as he slid inside.

Rolen pulled back, watching Kantou's face as he clasped Kantou's ass and, slowly but firmly, drew Kantou into him. His eyes darkened with mingled pain and pleasure as Kantou penetrated deeper, feeling Rolen's muscles grip him so firmly it was all he could do to let Rolen set the pace. Rolen's mouth dropped open, slack with desire. "Oh," he breathed, "more. I want more. Give me all of it."

A stab of pain wrenched Kantou's heart. He'd dreamed those words, so many times—but in his dreams it had been Soleyla who uttered them, Soleyla who lay beneath him, hungry for his fullness.

Rolen reached up and wiped a tear from Kantou's cheek. "I know," he said gruffly, pulling Kantou down on top of him. "I know."

Kantou lay, his weight resting on Rolen's chest, his cock buried almost to the hilt in the scorching embrace of Rolen's ass. No, it wasn't Soleyla below him—but the hunger inside him no longer cared. The ache in his balls was almost agony as he shifted, feeling Rolen move below him. Closing his eyes, he heard Rolen whisper, "Please. Please, Kantou, fuck me."

It wasn't Soleyla's voice, but Kantou obeyed.

Rolen moaned as Kantou flexed his hips, pushing the last few inches of that huge, thick cock inside him. Nothing had ever felt vaguely like this. Slowly, steadily, it invaded him, filling him until it felt as if he would burst with the sensation. His own erection pulsed, teased by Kantou's firm abs as the younger man rocked carefully, decreasing and then increasing the pressure inside Rolen's passage, letting him adjust to the size of his cock.

God, it was huge! Tossing his head, Rolen moaned in an ecstasy he'd never imagined. His balls were squeezed painfully between their bodies, and he tightened his legs, pulling Kantou even harder against him, pushing up to increase the friction against his throbbing cock. As he felt Kantou sliding in and out, a strange, yearning hunger, foreign yet undeniable, seized him. Snaking his hand down, he wrapped his fingers around his shaft, and as Kantou pushed himself up onto his arms, Rolen grinned and spread his legs wide.

"Yes," he hissed. "Oh yes. Fuck me. Fuck me hard."

Rearing up like a stallion, Kantou grabbed Rolen's thighs and shoved them wider.

Kantou watched as Rolen, pinned below him, worked his fist up and down his thick shaft, his eyelids falling closed in sensual delight. The curved head seemed to strain between his fingers, and Kantou could see his come-hole gaping in anticipation.

"Please," Rolen repeated, as with one hand Kantou snagged the oil, drizzling it over Rolen's cock, then over his own, feeling the tension mount as his shaft slid freely in and out of the man below him. "Please, Kantou."

His cock swelled even further, buried in Rolen's ass, stretching it wider, and Rolen bucked below him, impaling himself, driving Kantou deeper. Rolen's black hair tangled as he tossed his head, moaning deliriously, and his hand savaged his cock, pumping the shaft with delicious abandon.

Something crumbled inside Kantou—a dream, perhaps—and he felt, as if for the first time, the fire in his loins, heard the blood roaring in his ears. He wanted to *fuck*, blindly, heedlessly, wanted to drown the desolation inside him in sensation, wanted the oblivion of the orgasm building rapidly in his balls.

Rolen writhed, impatient, and Kantou closed his eyes, feeling nothing but the blazing heat of greedy, grasping flesh surrounding him. Nothing existed but the need to pound into the oil-slicked tightness of Rolen's ass, over and over, yanking all the way back out to send his cock slamming like a spear into Rolen's hot, waiting hole.

His breath sped up, matching time with his thrusts, and the agony in his balls grew, spreading like wildfire down his thighs, into his belly, until he was ablaze with nothing but lust, nothing but the need to pound, and pound, and pound . . .

He threw his head back, groaning—and saw Soleyla standing, just inside the tent-flap, her face gray with shock. Then her eyes went suddenly black, deep, burning with a fury that froze Kantou's blood.

CHAPTER FOUR

Caught in an ecstasy he could never have imagined, Rolen moaned in anticipation as he felt Kantou freeze above him. He shoved his hips upward, sinking that glorious cock deep inside him, feeling his arousal tightening to an almost unimaginable peak. One more stroke was all it would take, one more rough, punishing thrust of Kantou's thick cock . . .

Then Kantou wrenched out of him, leaving a throbbing, aching emptiness where his rock-hard warmth had been. Rolen gasped in shock, and his eyes flew open just in time to see Soleyla, her face twisted in a murderous snarl, seize Kantou by the hair and hurl him across the tent. She leaped at Rolen, drawing her sword, and Rolen threw himself to one side as the blade came whistling down.

"Bastard!" she shrieked as Rolen dove for his sword, which he'd left leaning against a chair. Soleyla kicked the chair flying, and the sword clattered out of reach. Rolen rolled under her vicious swipe, hearing it whoosh past him. His hand closed on the pommel of his sword, and he twisted, getting his feet under him. Metal clashed against metal as he leaped up, catching her downstroke on the flat of his sword.

Rolen was only distantly aware of Kantou's shouts as he and Soleyla swayed in a clinch, their blades scraping against each other as they pressed for the advantage. Gods, she was strong! Her muscles bulged with berserker fury as she leaned into him, her teeth bared in a feral, inhuman grin.

At her expression, Rolen felt the first icy trickle of fear.

Kantou was shrieking, grabbing at Soleyla's leg in an

attempt to separate them. Tears poured down his cheeks. Contemptuously, she kicked him off, and Rolen snatched at the opportunity to gain some distance. He sprang to the far side of the bed and spun, watching Soleyla narrowly.

She turned to stalk him, her eyes glittering in the growing light like flaring emeralds, and the realization hit Rolen like a slap. Despite the fact that she was glaring right at him, she wasn't seeing him. Not really—not *him*, Rolen. All she saw was rage.

His apprehension was confirmed by the way she'd tossed Kantou aside like a rag doll. Night after night, Rolen had felt her roll away from him, and had roused himself long enough to see her draw Kantou close, her hands—even in sleep—moving over him with a tenderness that amazed Rolen.

Until today, Soleyla had never known sexual jealousy. How could she? Men were slaves, no more, used when wanted, ignored when not. Now, caught in the viselike grip of an emotion she had no experience with, probably didn't even have a *name* for, Soleyla could easily kill Kantou without even recognizing him.

Rolen swallowed with a throat suddenly dry with fear.

And who, a voice asked inside his head, *brought this situation about?*

He'd only been trying to comfort Kantou! Waking in the night to hear his sobs . . .

It wasn't you he was crying for.

No. It wasn't. Unused to the sting of self-recrimination, Rolen almost missed the deadly swipe Soleyla loosed at him. He sprang back, protesting against that voice in his head, *I only wanted to help him!*

Did you? Did you really?

Rolen flushed even as he brought his sword up to block Soleyla's thrust. No, that *wasn't* all he'd wanted. Trapped by the flurry of blows she rained on him, Rolen turned at bay—and found himself face to face with emotions he was embarrassed to claim.

Yes, all right, he *had* wanted to comfort Kantou. But hadn't there been, buried deep inside him, the knowledge that he'd be taking something from Soleyla? Paying her back for —

For what, Rolen? What did she actually do to you?

She'd *used* him, he snarled inwardly. Used him like those others had used his men, until they cried and crawled like animals at the feet of their captors, begging for release. And Soleyla had *dared* to suggest he submit himself to the same treatment!

His sword clanged off Soleyla's with renewed fury. But the small inward voice penetrated his rage, cool and distinct.

Are your people not worth it, Rolen? Their freedom, their very lives? Do you know *what you're up against?*

Rolen slumped inwardly, bludgeoned into honesty. No. He didn't. But he was furious at what had been done to his men — and, he admitted, terrified to his very bones of the plan she'd suggested.

So he'd taken it out on her, all of it, in the only way he could — by having sex with Kantou.

Mortified, he sprang beyond Soleyla, putting himself between her and Kantou, who cowered now against the wall of the tent, watching them. "All right!" he shouted as Soleyla came at him, her sword dancing in the air before her. Dropping his guard, he drew himself erect. Better he die than Kantou.

Yes, he thought, *better to die here, now, than . . .*

But even as the words formed in his mind, even as Soleyla was lunging at him, her sword raised for the kill, he heard himself repeat, his voice hard and clear as the toll of an iron gong, "All right, Soleyla. I'll do it."

The man lowered his sword, Soleyla saw, leaving her a perfect opening. Something in her laughed in feral delight, and her sword flitted like a bird through the air — a bird with razor-like wings.

Then a figure leaped between them, screaming, his arms spread wide to protect the other man. Snarling, Soleyla jabbed her sword forward —

— and froze as its tip left a thin, bloody cut across Kantou's chest.

Kantou.

Her Kantou.

For a moment, the world went gray. Soleyla's stomach heaved. Her sword clattered to the floor as she stared, panting. Kantou shrank back against Rolen, and Soleyla saw the Antorean's hand come up to rest reassuringly on his shoulder.

A sickly flood of wrath twisted through her, black and poisonous. So that was how it was then. Soleyla nodded, regarding them both with a contempt so thick it could find no words. She'd seen them, face to face, bodies entwined, so wrapped up in each other they hadn't even heard her enter.

Nothing would ever make her forget that sight.

She felt her face set like stone as she studied Rolen. His face was ashen — *fear?* she wondered. *Afraid I'd kill his little plaything?* Rolen could have him. She didn't care. She spun on her heel and headed for the tent flap.

"Soleyla!" Rolen called after her. Something like desperation tightened his voice. "Soleyla, I said I'd do it!"

She turned back, sneering. The sight of them, practically clinging to each other in fright, sickened her. "Fine," she spat. "Get your men together. We leave tonight."

Then she was gone.

Six days later, Soleyla crouched behind a boulder at the lip of a ridge. Far in the distance, behind another stony rise, the spire of the comm tower gleamed dully in the gray, murky light. Below it, as yet unseen, lay the compound hurriedly erected some three months before by the advance team, slapped together from prefab parts imported whole through the main portal.

It was that portal which worried Soleyla. The smaller personnel portal could be readily defended — but the large utility portals, broad enough to drive a field engine through, could disgorge a platoon of support troops in a wave that would whirl her small band away like a twig in a flood. If she couldn't disable it . . . Scowling, Soleyla sank back to her knees, feeling muddy water soak through her pants.

Cold and unpleasant as it had made the long, torturous trek through the mountains, the weather suited Soleyla's mood. Gray, heavy with constant moisture, the foggy air had swirled around them, hiding them from any chance observation. The circuitous path she and Kantou had taken through the peaks, laying down relays for the comm system, had looped slowly north, far out of the more direct path by which Rolen, grim and silent, had led them through the mists. Even within the steely shadows of her rage, Soleyla had noted — and been impressed by — his knowledge of the mountains and ability to find the safest, most hidden paths through them.

He knelt beside her now, his scowling gaze fixed on that high, pointed tower. Twice during the first day of the hike, he'd tried to talk to her, his jaw clenched as he muttered something that might have been an attempt at apology — Soleyla didn't listen long enough to find out. Both times, she'd cut him off by the simple expedient of turning her back and walking away. After that, he'd lapsed into a sullen silence, punctuated only by the briefest of commands to his men.

For all their inexperience with warfare, Soleyla couldn't fault the Antorean's discipline. They had marched sixteen agonizing hours a day without complaint, rising wordlessly in the drizzling dawns to gather their packs and march again.

Even in her first, murderous fury at Rolen, it had never occurred to Soleyla to go back on her vow, and as she'd watched them, their faces set as they pushed themselves day by day through the torturous terrain, she was glad of that.

These men were as tough, as determined, as any Guardian. They deserved better than the enslavement the League had planned for them — enslavement, or extermination. Marching among them, Soleyla had felt a shred of the same fierce pride she'd seen in Rolen's eyes, and knew that, whatever lay ahead, whatever happened between herself, Rolen, and Kantou, never again would she be able to look at a man and see only a slave.

When she'd spied Kantou, though, standing among their assembled ranks the night they'd prepared to depart, Soleyla had raged at him. Trembling beneath her castigation, he had nevertheless held himself straight, only his white, stricken face and the tears trembling at the corners of his eyes betraying how her words cut him. A fierce, ugly sort of gladness had flowed through her, reveling in his agony, but when Rolen had intervened, she'd stopped, whirling away to stalk off into the gathering dusk.

He wasn't hers anymore. He was free — free to do whatever he liked, even die, spitted on a Guardian sword. Soleyla refused to examine too closely the wrench of pain that clenched her gut at the possibility.

All through the long trek she'd been aware of him, like a cloud at the corner of her vision, shadowing her. Stolidly, he'd hiked among the others, uncomplaining, always at a certain distance, defiantly ignoring the glares she occasionally threw over her shoulder. She could *feel* him, a constant irritant, like sand in a wound, as he struggled to maintain the grueling pace set by the larger, sturdier Antoreans.

Was he so devoted to Rolen then, that he would kill himself to follow him? Fine. Let him. She didn't care.

But some small part of her mind noted that every night when he lay down, it was never near the Antorean leader.

Soleyla backed away from the ridge top, sliding down on hands and knees until the spire had dropped from view, then stood. There was nothing more to see from here. If Valda had 'ported in more Guardians, then so be it. Whatever enemies they faced on the morrow, this was their one, their only, shot. There would be no second chance.

Behind her, she heard the small click of stones as Rolen followed her down from their perch. The men were encamped in the next valley over, concealed in the maze of caves and tunnels that pocked the weathered stone, resting and regaining their strength for the coming battle. When she heard Rolen clearing his throat, Soleyla lengthened her strides — not from any hurry to return to the men, merely from a wish to avoid conversation with Rolen. They both knew what had to be done tomorrow. What else was there for them to discuss?

"Soleyla." She heard his heavy footfalls behind her and quickened her pace. Not fast enough — his hand closed on her wrist, spinning her around. At her snarl, his eyes widened, but he didn't release her arm. "Soleyla, please!"

"What?" She spat the word at him, sneering inwardly as she saw him flinch. His face was pale underneath his tan, drawn and haggard with lack of sleep — and fear? He dropped his gaze, his throat working convulsively as he swallowed.

"Soleyla, I . . ." He raised his eyes again, and the panicked plea in them held her still. "Tomorrow, I . . . Soleyla, I can't do it!"

Her face set like stone. She knew what she was asking of him, and Soleyla had to admit he had every reason to be terrified. But without that distraction . . . Making her voice as stern as if she were speaking to a raw recruit, she snapped, "Yes, you can. You have to. Look at me!" she barked as his gaze slid away. He jerked upright at her tone.

Soleyla gave him a small, reassuring smile. *Forget that he's Rolen*, a small part of her whispered, the part of her that had been born, bred, and trained to command. *Forget Kantou, and everything that lies between you. This is a soldier, on the eve of the most dangerous mission of his life. If he fails . . .*

"You will not fail," Soleyla said, her voice steady and sure. She saw her words and the faith they expressed sink home, saw his shoulders relax just a fraction. "These are your people. Your planet. And you will do whatever you must to save them. I've watched you, Rolen. You can do it."

He swallowed again and nodded, his expression still frightened, but resolute. He drew himself up, towering over her, once again the massive, canny leader who had once backed her against a cliff, fighting *her*, a Guardian captain, to a standstill. At the memory, an involuntary grin stretched her lips, surprising her. If this man couldn't do what she'd asked of him and survive, no man could.

Rolen grinned back, a savage, reckless gleam in his eyes. Yes, strange as it was, this was a man worth fighting beside. Soleyla pitied the woman who tried to make a slave of *him*.

Which led her, of course, to Kantou. Soleyla's grin froze, then slid into a scowl. She started to turn away, but Rolen grabbed her again, his strong hands gripping her shoulders, forcing her to look up at him. "Soleyla," he said, his eyes burning down at her with an intensity that had nothing playful in it now. "Soleyla, if I'm going to do this tomorrow, I want you to do something for me."

She shifted in his grip, uncomfortable beneath that fierce, earnest gaze. "No promises. What?"

"Talk to Kantou."

At that, she flicked her arm up, breaking his hold on her shoulder, and spun away. When he tried to grab her again, she backhanded him, feeling a grim satisfaction at the thud of bone against bone. He staggered back, then caught his balance, glaring at her from under that thick black hair. He shook his head, studying her. "You stupid, stubborn woman."

"How dare you." Her voice was flat, low, dangerous.

"I?" Rolen laughed, one short, hard bark which had nothing to do with merriment. "I'm going to die down there tomorrow. I'll dare whatever I damn well like."

"Good." Striding past him, Soleyla headed for the encampment.

"Damn you, woman!" Rolen lunged after her, spinning her around. Struggling, she tripped him, and together they went down, rolling on the ground until Rolen pinned her, grinding her wrists against the stony earth. Panting, he glared down at her. She glared back, furious.

"What will you do now, Rolen? Try to rape me again?"

Turning his head, he spat in disgust. "I wouldn't lower myself." He sat up, releasing her, and Soleyla lay, surprised, rubbing one bruised wrist.

"You really *are* an idiot, you know," he continued. "He worships the ground you walk on, and you won't even see it." Shoving himself to his feet, Rolen stood for a moment, looking out over the rugged peaks of his world. "Love is a strange, strange thing." Soleyla wasn't sure if he was talking to her, or to the mountains around them. "You'll gladly kill yourself for something that doesn't even know you exist."

He glanced down at her again, extended a hand almost absently, and pulled her to her feet. "Talk to him, Soleyla," he repeated. "He loves you."

Shoulders square, his fears once again under control, he strode away. But it was a long, long time before Soleyla followed.

CHAPTER FIVE

The drizzle, which had thickened and thinned over the past six days without ever fully stopping, settled with the dusk to a light, steady rain. Under its soft continuous patter, the men of Rolen's tribe, the sturdy descendants of League renegades, sat, huddled, or stood near the mouths of the interlocking caves, looking out over the shadowed, muddy, rain-obscured valley. Every man there, Soleyla knew, felt the weight of his own death, as steadily and inexorably as the damp that seeped into their bones. She felt it herself. But there was no sense of wavering, no hesitation to be perceived among the grim faces enduring the onslaught of night.

For many of them, it was their last night. Win or lose, the death toll would be horrific. If they lost, it would be annihilation—not only of them, but of their lovers, children, and families they'd left behind. For those stakes, Soleyla knew, not a man among them would turn back. She was, she admitted, proud of them.

She was seated alone, in a small chamber opening off the main cavern where most of the men had gathered. No fires flickered, not even deep in the tunnels behind her. A cleft in the rocks gave her a narrow view of the valley, and as night deepened her eyes ceaselessly scanned it, senselessly searching for some point her gaze could fix on, some landmark to cling to in the damp, trackless night. Somewhere behind the clouds a full moon shone, so that not even the dark was absolute. Everything wavered. Stones blurred into sky, sky melted into mountain, everything was mutable, featureless, incomprehensible.

He worships the ground you walk on.

Kantou's beautiful face, clenched with a need she'd never seen there before, so rapt in Rolen's body he hadn't even heard her enter . . .

You stupid, stubborn woman.

His voice, screaming as he leapt in front of Rolen, arms outspread, ready to die to protect the man he'd just been . . .

Just been . . .

Say it, Soleyla!

Just been *fucking.* Her mouth twisted into a snarl. Was she supposed to *forget* that? Just put it aside as if it meant nothing? Easy for Rolen to say — Rolen who'd held Kantou in his arms, drawing Kantou down to him, kissing him, feeling his cock inside him . . .

Talk to him, Soleyla.

Talk to him? She could barely stand to *look* at him. If she could, she would scrape the memory of his face from her mind, the way he'd looked, lying beside her, relaxed in sleep, unguarded, vulnerable . . .

Her eyes scanned the night, ceaseless, restless. She hardly noticed the tears coursing down her cheeks.

What was she supposed to do? Go and find him? Prostrate herself before him and beg his forgiveness? For what? For throwing away her commission, her future, for turning traitor against her own people in the quest to set him free? And what did he do with that freedom?

He fucked Rolen.

He loves you.

But he fucked Rolen.

Worships the ground you . . .

He *fuckedRolen*, damn it!

Soleyla slammed her head back against the rock, sending lights bursting before her eyes. Pain seared through her, and she clung to it, grateful for any fixed point in the internal whirlwind that buffeted her mind. Gasping, she swiped impatiently at the damp on her cheeks, only dimly aware she'd been crying. Was still crying. Shudders shook her, and she raised a hand to her mouth, struggling to contain her sobs.

Then a voice spoke behind her, and her grief congealed into an icy, solid hate.

"My lady."

Had he come to gloat? To see the mighty Soleyla Devarian, reduced to tears like a man? She would not give him the satisfaction. Raising her chin, she stared out into the darkness — though what there was for her to see out there was a question she could not ever have answered. Her voice, she was pleased to note, was cold and steady. "Get out."

"My lady, please."

Swiveling her head, confident he wouldn't be able to see her tears, Soleyla stared haughtily. Kantou was no more than a smudge against the darkness, an outline against the blackness behind him.

"I said get out."

"My lady . . . Soleyla . . ."

A shriek rose in her throat, burning. Soleyla clenched her jaw, fighting it. How far, in the moist air, would such a shriek carry? Would she betray their position for the satisfaction of screaming at Kantou? Rigidly, she spoke, her voice low and deadly.

"Leave, Kantou. Now."

In the dim gray light, she saw him sink to his knees, his head bent, his face obscured by the fall of his thick, straight hair. In the shadowy dark, it glimmered like cobwebs, like raw silk. Her hand, itching to stroke it, closed into a fist instead.

Uncurling herself, Soleyla rose to her full height, feeling adrenaline pumping through her legs, her arms, tightening the heavy muscles developed by years of combat, rushing down her limbs as if in preparation for a battle. She could feel the bloodlust growing in her, the desire to hurt, to maim, to rend . . .

"I will warn you one last time, Kantou. Leave. Or I will break every vow I ever made to you."

He didn't move.

Fury shot through her, and her body quivered as she strode forward, bringing her hand up to cuff him. As she approached, he raised his head, unflinching. His eyes were huge in his pale face, wide, waiting. Trembling with rage, she stood over him, poised to strike.

"Please, Soleyla. Beat me. Hit me. I don't care." His voice was soft, desperate, pleading. "Only don't, don't ignore me anymore."

At his tone, the fury in her climbed another notch, making her head spin with the urge, the bone-deep *need*, to smash him, batter him, *break* him until he crawled, whimpering, at her feet. Contemptuously, she kicked him, hard, in the chest, sending him sprawling backward across the jagged floor.

Tears started from his eyes and yet he didn't roll away, didn't raise his arms to protect himself. He simply lay there, his eyes fixed mutely on her as she loomed over him, one booted foot poised to smash in his beautiful, treacherous face.

You are not your mother, my lady.

Merkun's voice rang in her ears, as clearly as if he stood next to her in the darkness. Soleyla froze, jolted, it felt, out of herself. For a moment she stood, seeing herself, foot raised over Kantou, ready to stomp him, to shatter the bones of his face into a bloody pulp.Seeing the black, poisonous pride inside her like an infection, a sickness her mother had long ago succumbed to.

And he would let her, Soleyla realized. Making no move to defend himself, with no protest, no recrimination, not even judgment, Kantou would have let her.

Spinning from him, Soleyla leapt for the cave's opening

just in time, collapsing onto her knees as she vomited, over and over, smelling the sickly tang of bile until the steady fall of rain washed it away.

The floor of the cave was cold under her cheek, and rough. Outside, the rain pattered on, soft and unfailing. Feeling as drained and empty as a bleached piece of driftwood, Soleyla pulled herself stiffly to a seat, her back against the stone.

There was something near her in the darkness. Something warm, unmoving, so close all she had to do was reach out her hand to touch it. "Kantou," she said, and that was all. That was enough. He came to her, silently, and laid his head in her lap. Wearily, she stroked his hair, finding comfort even in her exhaustion in the thick, silken feel of its heavy smoothness, sliding through her fingers like water.

He loves you.

All she could feel was a stunned sort of surprise, a dumb, animal gratitude at a gift so huge, so incomprehensible, she could do nothing but accept it. She felt him shift, sighing, under her caress. His arms wrapped around her thighs, holding her as if he was afraid she'd disappear.

"Soleyla," he whispered, not a question, just her name. He said it again, as if the word alone were a benediction, a source of strength and comfort. "Soleyla."

A slight, tired smile curved her lips. What could she do? How could she resist that? Cupping her hand under his chin, she lifted gently, and he rose to his knees beside her. Tilting her head against the wall, she gazed at him, saw tears trembling at the corners of his eyes.

"I thought . . . I thought you didn't want me anymore," he whispered, his voice cracking with remembered grief.

Soleyla stared, bemused. "Why?"

"You . . . you never spoke to me. Barely even looked at me. You wouldn't . . . wouldn't let . . ." He faltered, his gaze dropping.

"Wouldn't what, Kantou?"

"You wouldn't let me make love to you. Not like that. Not the way you let Rolen . . ."

Soleyla straightened, reaching out to stroke Kantou's face. His eyes, gray and luminous, stared into hers, pain shining nakedly in their depths.

"You saw us?"

He nodded.

"Oh, Kantou," she breathed. Drawing him to her, she wrapped one arm around him. He dropped his head to her shoulder, cupping her other hand between his, running his fingers over it again and again as if to make sure it was real.

Soleyla kissed the top of his head, smelling the clean, sweet scent of his hair. "You still don't understand, do you? Everything I do—*everything*, Kantou—is for you."

He tilted his head back, studied her, confused. "But . . . you let him inside you, and you never . . ."

Soleyla almost laughed as she finally understood. It was a bitter jest, though, and her jaw clenched, twisting her smile. As Kantou shifted, drawing back, afraid he'd offended her, she shook her head reassuringly, and pulled him back. "No, Kantou. It's not you I'm angry at."

He was silent for a moment. She could feel his heartbeat, soft and even, beneath her palms.

Then he asked, "But why wouldn't you let me?"

"Because, Kantou . . ." And this time she *did* chuckle, her amusement running like a warm thread through the worn, faded cloth of her emotions. "I wanted it to be special. Private. Something that was just between us. I wasn't about to share it with Rolen."

"Oh."

Soleyla smiled again, hearing in his voice the same chagrined realization she'd felt herself, a few moments earlier. And then grinned as she leaned her head against his, letting her lips brush gently against his ear. "Rolen's not here, Kantou."

His eyes widened, and he drew back, studying her. In the dim, lambent light she saw his throat work, swallowing, and felt her exhaustion fall away.

Her nerves tingled, suddenly aware of the cold, the damp night air, the hard rock beneath her. It was hardly the ideal place or time. But—and the knowledge returned to her in a rush that set her pulse leaping—it might be the only place and time they would ever have.

Never before had the thought of battle frightened her. But now, Soleyla quailed at the possibilities the coming day might bring. Was it worth it? She would happily risk her own life, would risk the lives of Rolen's men without a qualm—they were fighting for their own lives, and the lives of their loved ones, after all—but the idea of Kantou injured, Kantou killed, turned Soleyla's knees to water. She couldn't do it. She couldn't . . .

Kantou was touching her, his hands stroking her cheekbones, her lips, her hair. Something of her fear must have shown, for he whispered, "I'm not afraid, Soleyla. I'm not afraid of dying. The only thing I'm afraid of is losing you again."

She opened her mouth to speak, but he laid a gentle finger across her lips. "No. I won't stay behind. I won't wait, wondering, not knowing if you'll return to me. Not here, not back at the camp. Where you go, I go. Even into death. Promise me that, my lady."

Her eyes closed as his words pierced her, penetrating her heart. It ached, overburdened, so full of love she could find no answer but to kiss him, to cover his mouth with hers, taste the salt of his dried tears on his lips. She pulled him to her, hungry for the feel of his tongue in her mouth, the rush of saliva as their tongues met, seeking, exploring, sliding against and around each other to dart eagerly deep between the other's lips.

With a sigh that was half sob, Kantou dragged her against him, covering her face with kisses, clasping her tightly, as if he thought she might turn to mist and float away. His mouth grazed her chin, her cheeks, his breath ragged in her ear as he nuzzled her neck.

Soleyla's hands slid over him, caressing his strong, broad shoulders, his arms, rising to run through his hair. Her fingers clenched in the smooth, heavy strands as he opened her shirt, bent his head to her breast, and suckled with a blind, hungry, animalistic greed.

Heat exploded in her loins, raced along her limbs as his mouth worked at her, tugging, sucking, as if trying to fill the emptiness which had driven him, sharper than any lash, through the long, grueling, six-day trek. His hands came up to cup her breasts, squeezing them, lifting them toward his mouth which clamped first on one, then the other, tonguing and nibbling her aching, erect nipples, then closing around them, sucking her breast deep into his mouth.

Soleyla's hands slid over his arms, his shoulders, down his back as she arched her own, shoving her breasts into his seeking, teasing mouth. He nuzzled between them, his fingers tugging her nipples, pinching them as she gasped in pleasure. Sliding one hand behind her back, he lowered her gently to the hard floor. Unfastening her pants, he slid them downward, drew them off and threw them somewhere into the shadows. Soleyla panted, waiting, shivering slightly in the cold.

A warm, gentle hand closed around her ankle, trailed slowly up her calf. She quivered as it stroked the inside of her thigh, played delicately over the curling hair of her mons, then moaned, deep in her throat, as Kantou knelt between her legs, bending down to taste her.

His tongue licked at her opening, hungrily lapping her free-flowing juices. With a groan, he closed his mouth on her, flicking his tongue over her engorged clit. Soleyla spread her legs, letting him delve deeper, felt his tongue thrusting between her sensitive lips. Already she could feel heat rising within her, building toward a peak. His hands slid over her hips, her belly, caressing her full, firm breasts as his tongue danced along her clit, teasing her until she thrashed beneath him, her head tossing from side to side, murmuring senseless, half-formed words.

Kantou stopped, lifted his head, and she cried out in protest at the withdrawal of his tongue. As her hands fisted in his hair, shoving his head back down, she felt his lips curve into a brief, exultant smile. Wrapping her legs around him, she crushed him to her, forcing his face hard against her sex.

He sighed in contentment, the warm, rich sound vibrating against her. Then, seizing her breasts in hands that were suddenly rough and insistent, he clamped his mouth around her clit, sucking and nipping and lapping it with a craving that drove her, shuddering, over the brink. Light exploded behind her eyelids as her entire body strained, her back arching off the floor, her fists closing convulsively in his hair, toward the throbbing, pulsing point between her thighs.

Soleyla came back to awareness to find him stretched beside her, his head resting on her shoulder as he stroked her lightly, her face, her neck, her full, aching breasts. His gaze, wide and wondering, followed the trail of his hands, as if he was both amazed and humbled by this chance to touch her. Soleyla quivered as he drew his long, agile fingers in a path down her belly, circling her navel playfully, tickling her.

"Stop that," she whispered. His finger hesitated, then resumed its circular course. "Kantou, I said stop it!" But her voice burbled with laughter, and so he ignored her. Grinning, she shook her head and lay back, content to let him fondle her however he liked. Outside, the rain fell in a soft, ceaseless, tuneless song that seemed to wrap them, warm and inter-twined, in a small, secret space. Nothing could touch, threaten or divide them behind the rain's protective veil.

Kantou lifted her hand, interweaving her fingers with his, and she turned her head to look at him. Gently, as lightly as dew settling on a flower, he kissed her—her forehead, her closed eyelids, her mouth. She parted her lips, felt his tongue slide, shy and hesitant, between them.

She touched it with her own, then drew back, gazing at him, tracing the line of his thick arched eyebrows, running her finger along one high curved cheekbone, playing it over his full lower lip. "My beautiful Kantou . . ."

"Am I?" His eyes were dark, shadowed, yearning still.

What words would it take, Soleyla wondered, to fill that yearning, to chase away the uncertainty in those smoky gray eyes?

No, not words. Soleyla paused as understanding blos-somed within her. No words could convey what he most longed to hear. She grabbed his hair at the base of his neck, roughly, saw his eyes fly open, startled. Placing her hand on his shoulder, she pushed him down onto his back. "Spread your legs," she commanded, and saw his face suffuse with arousal as he obeyed. His enormous erection brushed his stomach, its tip covering his navel. Soleyla felt a fresh throb of anticipatory heat, deep inside her. But first . . .

She grasped his thighs, forcing them up and out. Kantou lifted his hips, giving her access to his ass—but that wasn't what she wanted. Not tonight. Grinning wickedly, she wrapped one hand around his shaft, so thick her fingers didn't come close to circling it. She tilted it up, hearing Kantou gasp as she lowered her head. Then she wrapped her lips around it.

The sensation was intoxicating. Hot, throbbing, tasting

slightly of salt, his firm, engorged head filled her mouth, her jaw straining as she sought to encompass all of it. Gods, what would it feel like inside her? She flicked her tongue over its small, gaping slit, feeling him jerk and tremble, tasting the bead of come forming just inside. Prodding, she darted her tongue, over and over, against that sweet, tiny hole, hearing Kantou's breath go ragged as his whole body tensed, quivering, below her.

Straining her mouth wider, she sucked, drawing all of his head inside. Her teeth scraped lightly against the thick, meaty rim, and she wrapped her lips over it and clamped down, hard. Kantou arched like a drawn bow, his hips rising off the rock as she swirled her tongue over and over the smooth velvet firmness of his cockhead. He whimpered, and she felt her body throb in response to his need.

Tightening her grip on his shaft, she raised her head, her gaze seeking his face. It was flushed, lax with desire, his eyes heavy-lidded and smoky. "I told you once, Kantou," Soleyla growled, her voice low and thrilling, "I would have you. Where, when, and as I liked."

"Yes, my lady." Panting, he whispered the words.

"Look at me, Kantou!"

His eyes opened wide.

"Say it, Kantou."

Smiling inwardly, she watched his Adam's apple bob as he swallowed, then licked his dry lips. "You will have me, my lady. When, where, and as you like."

"Because you are mine, Kantou. Mine, and no one else's." He lay watching her, his lips parted soundlessly. She reached up, yanked his hair, pulling his head upward. "Say it, Kantou!"

"I am yours, Soleyla. Yours to use however you wish." His eyes, glowing with exaltation, watched her face.

"Good." She released him. "Get on your knees." He did,

his erection jutting, enormous, before him. Soleyla leaned back, sprawling lazily on the ground.

"Now fuck me, Kantou."

He looked at her, a wild, surprised hope burning in his eyes. She grinned. "You heard me. Slave."

His head dropped back on his strong, graceful neck, and she heard him sigh, long and low. Slowly, disbelieving, he brought his hands to her thighs, running his palms down the length of them, then curling between, spreading them wide. As Rolen once had done, he looked down at her, gazing raptly at the juice-slicked folds of her sex. His cock throbbed, huge, rigid, so engorged the skin was stretched to a hard, shiny surface.

He raised his gaze once more to her face, and Soleyla saw tears shining in his eyes. As he lowered himself above her, his tears slid free, gliding down his cheeks to fall, warm and soft, onto her chest.

"Oh, my lady," he breathed. "Oh, Soleyla."

And with that last, whispered syllable, his cock nudged against her opening. Soleyla spread her thighs wider, wrapping her legs about his lean waist. Her pussy ached, eager for his thickness, and she arched against him, feeling his tip slowly work its way in. Gods, it was huge! It pressed against her, filling her, stretching her wide in a way that made her gasp with pleasure. Nothing, no man, had felt remotely like this and — she realized, swallowing slightly — the head wasn't even all the way inside her yet.

He paused, his arms trembling as he held himself above her, his thick straight hair falling like a veil around her face, sliding over her breasts like silk. His jaw hung slightly open, his lips parted, his eyes closed in fiercely controlled ecstasy. She reached up, stroked his face, and he looked down at her, his eyes full of an emotion so clear, so radiant, that for a moment Soleyla was abashed.

59

How could she not have seen how he loved her, wanted her, needed her? She was every bit the stubborn fool Rolen had called her. She had wasted so much time, time she could have spent, just like this, with Kantou poised above her, quivering with desire.

She slid her hands up his trembling arms, laid them gently on his broad scarred back. Firmly, she said, "I want you inside of me, Kantou. All of you. Now."

Kantou closed his eyes, feeling tears stream down his face. Why now did he cry, now when everything he'd ever wanted, everything he'd hoped for, was here? But as he slid himself deep into Soleyla's throbbing tightness, Kantou sobbed at the sweetness of the sensation.

Warm and slick, her passage closed around him as he pressed gently, easing his shaft deeper inside her. How he had dreamed of this! Quivering, he paused, feeling desire race along his cock. He could, Kantou thought wildly, come right this second.

Slowly, carefully, he backed out an inch, feeling the hot clasp of her opening squeeze his shaft. He was hers, body and soul. Now and forever. Whatever Soleyla wanted, he would do. Whatever she commanded. Every sensation she made him feel, every twinge of pain and desire, was ecstasy beyond his deepest fantasies. She would drive him, Kantou knew, to the heights of lust, riding him to an unimaginable peak.

A sense of exaltation filled him, mingling with the ache of his balls into a rapture he had no words for. He could only whisper, his voice ragged with desire, "Soleyla. Oh, my lady."

He felt her shift below him, press up against his careful strokes, greedily thrusting her hips into the air. With a sob, Kantou tossed his head, feeling his hair slide like a heavy silken veil across his trembling shoulders, and pistoned himself down, deep into his lady's sweet, scorching wetness.

Soleyla moaned as she felt Kantou lunge, his control shattering, plunging his cock deep inside her in one swift, hard motion. Her head snapped back, and her core blazed with sudden heat, stretched wide by his thick, pulsating shaft. She felt him push deeper, felt his cock forcing its way through her entrance, aware of how her muscles gripped him, squeezing. And *still* he was not yet all the way in her.

"I thought I told you, Kantou," she growled, her voice low with menace. She could almost feel his balls contract in reaction, aching to spill their seed inside her. "I want it. All of it. Now!" Burying her fist in his hair, she yanked him downward, feeling his cock flex once inside her before he thrust himself home.

His pelvic bone ground against hers, mashing her clit. Her breasts were flattened against his heaving chest. His cock slammed deep, igniting a flare of lust so breathtaking, Soleyla felt her head spin.

It was enormous. Overwhelming. His cock filled her so completely Soleyla thought she might pass out from delight. Like velvet iron it stretched her open, possessing every inch of her. "Yes," she hissed, "oh yes, Kantou." She felt him stiffen above her, rigid with need, then shiver with delight as she ordered, her voice hard and demanding, "Now fuck me."

Slowly, he drew himself out, his cock swelling against the sides of her passage, until she felt the rim of his head drag against her lips. He stayed there, rocking, and she could feel her entrance squeezing his head, compressing it, crushing the rim as it popped back inside her. A roaring, aching emptiness flared inside her, and she grabbed his hips, dragging him forward, hearing him moan as he sank in to the hilt. She tightened her muscles, gripping him, and he whimpered, his head pressed against her neck, fighting for control.

"Oh, you like that, Kantou."

"Yes," he hissed. "I like it, my lady."

"Then fuck me, Kantou. Fuck me hard. Fuck me till it hurts."

"Oh, God," he breathed, and lifted himself, shuddering. His eyes were almost black with need as he reared above her. He drew himself back, then thrust down, hard, splitting her open, his pelvic bone grinding against her swollen clit. "Again," she commanded. "Faster."

With a wild, snorting sigh, he lunged back again, then obeyed, his hips straining as he slammed into her, again and again, filling her in a way no man ever had. Soleyla moaned deliriously as she felt him swell further, impossibly huge, his club-like cock pounding into her. Suddenly, he rocked back onto his haunches, grabbed her ass and dragged her up with him, so her legs were wrapped around his waist. Kantou's face clenched with mingled agony and delight as he wrenched her legs up, over his shoulders, sending his cock drilling into her in one hard, punishing thrust.

She saw Kantou's gaze fixed on her breasts as they jiggled, bounced by the strength of his thrusts. Wantonly, she rubbed them, squeezing the nipples, heard his breath hiss between his teeth as she tweaked them. "Harder?" she asked and felt a fresh spurt of wetness slick her passage as he nodded mutely, his eyes huge and round as he watched her seize her nipples and pinch them fiercely between her strong fingers.

"Oh God, Soleyla," he gasped. Then his breath caught as his whole body tensed upward, freezing on the edge of ejaculation. Grabbing his arms, Soleyla pulled herself up so that she straddled his thighs, his cock buried, rigid, inside her. His hands slid under her ass, cupping her cheeks, spreading them, and she could feel the hot, pulsing weight of his balls against her rectum. She pushed downward, grinding them between her ass and his strong thighs, and heard Kantou groan. "Oh, yes, my lady. Harder."

Rubbing her mound against the taut plane of his abs, Soleyla raised herself above him, then pistoned down, spearing herself on his huge, rock-hard shaft. Her ass slapped his balls, and she felt him buck, his cock throbbing inside her.

"Please," he begged, "please."

Faster, harder, she rode him, her clit mashed between them, savaging his balls with each punishing thrust. His head fell back, his breath raking through his throat, his hands dragging her down, harder, slamming her against him. She felt his muscles tense, and lust coiled inside her, tight and voracious, demanding all of him, his pain, his ecstasy, his complete submission.

She raked her teeth over his throat, felt his cock pulse as she twisted his nipples, heard a blank, white-hot roaring inside her skull. Her passage spasmed, gripping him tight as he thrust up so hard he lifted her clear off the floor, holding her aloft with only his hands and his huge, pounding cock. Her legs clenched around him, drawing him deep, and she felt every throb of his shaft as he came, exploding inside her in wave after searing wave, filling her until his juices ran down between them. And with one harsh, agonized groan, Kantou rammed himself deep and clung to her, shaking.

CHAPTER SIX

Slowly, tenderly, he lowered her to the ground. Soleyla whimpered as Kantou withdrew, wanting his cock inside her again, right now — right now and always. He bent over her, his long hair brushing her face, and kissed her gently. As he raised his head, Soleyla finally saw what his eyes looked like without any shadows. Clear and luminous, they gazed down at her, filled with a light like swift running water.

The air around them was gray, now, brightening slowly toward an overcast dawn. The clouds outside the cave's jagged opening were low, dense, iron gray. Soleyla pulled Kantou down, and he curled at her side, his head on her shoulder, one hand playing with her hair. Suddenly, the awareness of what this day would bring hung heavy around them.

"Kantou . . ." she started.

He shook his head, cutting her off. "No, my lady. I won't stay behind."

Soleyla sighed. "Then stick close to me, Kantou. I couldn't bear to lose you."

He lifted her hand, cupping it in his, and dropped a soft kiss in her palm. Around them, almost noiseless in the cool air, they heard the shift and fall of stones as Rolen's men climbed from the tunnels, assembling in the valley below.

Giving him one last kiss, Soleyla rose and dressed. She didn't look back as she stepped through the crevasse and clambered carefully to the valley floor, knowing full well Kantou would follow.

Fog swirled around her as she reached the bottom. Already

the men were trickling eastward, flitting in ones and twos up the far slope of the valley like wraiths between the rocks, making their way to the rendezvous she and Rolen had selected the day before.

Finally, she spied Rolen through the eddying mist. He was standing near Jerril, the towering blond giant who had helped him first abduct Soleyla, speaking earnestly in a low, tense voice. Jerril nodded, then grinned at Soleyla as she approached. He, too, had a Guardian sword of ancient manufacture sheathed at his waist, and Soleyla again felt a burst of kinship with those long-ago Guardians who had fled to this isolated planet. Such a man, she thought, looking at the tall, easygoing man with his ready smile, should never be a slave.

Rolen, following Jerril's gaze, nodded at Soleyla, then saw Kantou behind her. His eyebrows lifted questioningly, and Soleyla smiled, which was all the answer Rolen needed. "Good," he replied. "It's about time."

He gestured to the men moving out of the valley. "They'll be in position before sunrise."

"If any sun can rise in this murk," added Jerril.

The rain had finally stopped, but the air was full of the magnified sound of water, dripping from the rocks and the low stunted brush that grew between them. The morning felt chancy, thick with tension, or perhaps it was Soleyla's own uneasiness that made the lowering clouds seem so threatening. She nodded. "Better for us. Get them down to the ridge before this fog lifts. I'll unlock the gates in time for your attack."

Jerril looked at her, surprised. "Won't they notice?"

Soleyla gave him a hard grin. "They'll be otherwise occupied."

She saw Rolen's jaw clench at her words, and his hands tighten around the hank of rope he carried. He drew his sword, handing it to Jerril, and Soleyla could see the reluctance with which he released the pommel. Gripping Jerril's arm briefly in farewell, he turned away, not even watching as the massive blond man strode away, disappearing into the mist.

Soleyla watched him worriedly. Rolen's throat worked, but he said nothing, nor could she find any words, either of comfort or courage. After a moment, he started up the southern slope of the valley, his shoulders rigid with tension, his tread heavy and stern. Silently, Soleyla and Kantou followed.

Was it his imagination, Rolen wondered, or was the day actually growing darker? The sun must have cleared the horizon by now, but the overcast had thickened, and he had to strain to make out a path through the damp, slippery rocks. Twenty minutes later, with Soleyla and Kantou behind him, he reached a rude, hard packed path, churned to mud by the rain, curving along the base of the mountains.

"Flitter track," Soleyla said. "We'd better have the rope."

Rolen grimaced. He'd railed against this one part of the plan for hours that night in the tent. Perhaps, he admitted now, he'd fought against it so hard simply to avoid the part that *truly* terrified him. But to allow Soleyla to truss him like a captive, lead him bound and weaponless into the Guardian compound . . . He stood in grim silence as Soleyla looped the rope around his hands, then his neck, fashioning a deft slipknot that would choke him if he struggled.

"I'm trusting you, Guardian." His voice was low, terse.

Soleyla answered with an equally terse smile. "I know." Stepping back, she studied him a moment. Kantou watched anxiously from the side of the track. "All right. We'd better get you pretty. Do you want to do it, or shall I?"

Rolen felt his mouth twist in a crooked grin. "I'll do it myself, thanks." He dropped to his knees, then fell forward face first into the mud. When he rose, he was dripping.

Soleyla nodded. "All right. Let's go." Holding his rope like a leash, she led him down the track.

By the time they topped the last of the foothills and saw the League compound below, all three of them were sweaty, sticky, splattered with heavy, cloying mud. Soleyla cursed, shaking the stuff from her boots. The air had grown thicker, overladen with moisture, and the sky was black above the white comm tower which jutted like a spire toward the threatening clouds.

Rolen stood, eyes narrowed, studying the stronghold of his enemy, noting the high plasteel walls, the ranks of barracks buildings, the shimmering field of the utility portal, fully fifteen meters wide, clearly visible in the dank, murky air. His shoulders stiffened, and his head came up defiantly. Soleyla yanked the rope sharply, and he staggered forward. Rage flared within him, and he spun.

Soleyla hissed at him, livid. "They can *see* us, Rolen!"

Immediately, Rolen slumped, letting his head hang at a cowed, beaten angle. He was supposed to be a prisoner, damn it. It was a role that chafed worse than the rope around his neck. But it was, he knew, necessary.

She started down the slope, dragging him behind her. Rolen had to fight back the urge to rip the rope from her hands as he staggered in the slick mud. As the walls of the compound loomed over them, though, his irritation faded, overwhelmed by an icy, sickly dread.

He'd refused to think about what came next, knowing if he did, he'd simply bolt in terror. Now he was here, trussed like a rabbit. There was no escape, no turning back. He could feel eyes on him, watching from the top of the high white walls.

"Rolen," Soleyla muttered, keeping her voice low and moving her mouth as little as possible. "Remember. The second you can no longer pleasure them, they will kill you. If you can't get an erection, you're dead."

"Oh, thanks. That'll *really* help my performance."

"Listen!" she hissed. "Don't let them make you come. They will, if they can. They will use you over and over until you are so spent that—"

"Flitter!" Kantou warned, behind them. A second later, Rolen heard a low, thrumming buzz, and almost turned to face it. Soleyla gave a quick tug on the rope, warning him, and he kept walking, his shoulders slumped, his gaze on the ground.

The buzz grew to a whine as it approached, then dropped to a low, idling thrum. "Well, Captain Devarian," sneered a hard, mocking voice.

"Lieutenant Trika." Soleyla's voice was cold. Her pace lengthened.

Rolen risked a glance from under his thick black brows. They were approaching the gates with alarming rapidity. Alongside Soleyla, a strange metallic machine hovered, seemingly on thin air, keeping pace with her. On its back a Guardian sat, grinning down. Lieutenant Trika, Rolen assumed, and quickly dropped his gaze as she looked back at him.

He heard the gates swing open. Before he had time to react or to brace himself, he was inside, and the gates were closing behind him. Rolen swallowed with a throat suddenly far, far too dry.

The flitter's buzz shut off, and he heard the sound of booted feet approach. "What's this, Devarian? A present? Nice of you to bring us a toy, since you won't share yours." Behind him, Rolen heard Kantou shift nervously.

Fingernails scraped lightly over his broad, naked chest, and Rolen jumped. Laughter echoed around him. Panicked, he looked up to see women standing around in military gear, watching him with grinning, speculative expressions, all of them built on the same Amazonian scale as Soleyla. He lunged, and Soleyla yanked on the rope, dragging him, retching as the noose around his neck tightened to a chokehold, to his knees. Immediately, the pressure eased.

"That's Captain, Lieutenant, unless you want to be reported for insubordination."

"Oh, I think not, *Captain*." Trika's sneer made the title an epithet. "The commander's none too pleased with your little antics. No more than you are, I'd imagine, being posted to this muddy shithole with the rest of us grunts."

As she spoke, Trika crossed to Rolen. Now, closing her fist in his thick black hair, she yanked his head up, forcing him to look at her. Rolen recoiled as she ran her tongue over her lips.

"Get your paws off him, Lieutenant. This one's for Valda."

"Valda's already got a pleasure slave. Besides, she won't mind if we have a go." A rumble of amusement from the watching soldiers followed Trika's words.

"I said, get your hands off him!" Bristling, Soleyla moved between them, shielding Rolen from Trika's hateful leer. "This one's a spy. I caught him following me. He'll tell us where the Antoreans' encampment is — *if* you greedy bitches don't kill him first."

"Ahhh," sighed another voice behind Rolen, "surely you won't begrudge them a little recreation, Captain?" Rolen saw Soleyla stiffen. "And we already know where their camp is, Captain Devarian."

Soleyla turned, snapping to attention. "Commander Valda." For all her lack of height, the short, squarely-built woman before her radiated an aura of command. Sly rather than brilliant, tenacious as a bulldog, Valda had been her mother's first choice as High Commander of the Guardian forces — a choice which an appalled Senate had overridden, awarding the position instead to the then-General Amista, whose ingenious tactics had preserved the League during the first brutal attacks by the V'ranyii.

Behind her formal salute, Soleyla's mind raced. *Did* Valda know the camp's location? Or was she bluffing? Had their entire plan already been discovered? Watching the shorter, steel-haired woman, Soleyla kept her expression carefully neutral. "That's good news, Commander."

"Indeed, and we have you to thank for it."

Soleyla froze. Inside, her blood ran to ice, and she had to fight back the urge to draw her sword. If Valda already knew . . .

Why hadn't she made Kantou stay in the caves?

"I'm glad to have been of service, Commander—although I will confess I'm a little puzzled."

"Are you?" Valda turned her attention to Rolen, lifting his head and studying him as she continued. "It's quite simple. When the communication relays you were supposed to have been laying stopped coming online, I was afraid something had happened to you. So I sent a patrol out. They found the remains of your campsite, and no trace of you . . . and oddly enough, on the plain just one ridge over, they found these natives' camp. Really quite large, too, right out in the open."

Rolen stiffened in her grasp, and Soleyla, watching, could only pray.*Keep still, Rolen, on your life and all you love!*

Valda ran her hands over his massive shoulders. "He is a handsome one, isn't he?" She glanced at Soleyla, her eyes sharp. "Strange you should have been so close to their camp and not have seen it."

"I didn't cross the ridge. When I captured this one—" Soleyla shoved Rolen with her boot, sending him sprawling in the dirt—he'd looked ready to tear Valda's hands off with his teeth, "—I assumed you'd want to question him as soon as possible. Or does laying a comm grid for colonists who aren't even here yet take precedence over neutralizing the native population?"

The older woman bristled, her iron-gray hair falling away from her low, broad forehead as she tilted her head back to glare up at Soleyla. "I was of the understanding you had a distaste for neutralizing populations, Captain Devarian."

"Shall we say my mother's gentle instruction has shown me the error of my ways?"

They scowled at each other, but inwardly Soleyla sighed with relief. If Valda had already discovered their plan, she and Rolen would be dead by now. And Kantou . . .

It didn't bear thinking of. Valda was every bit as ruthless as her old barracks mate, Rachel Devarian.

Two peas in a pod, Soleyla thought. She could feel her lips wanting to twist into a snarl. Instead, she asked, hoping her voice sounded casual, "Did you wipe them out already, then?"

"No. The patrol, unlike you, followed its orders and reported back to me directly."

Trika, standing nearby, smirked, and Soleyla allowed herself to flush at the chastisement. They *had* to play this game out, had to calm Valda's suspicions enough to let her get near the gate . . .

"But we will. Soon. Be sure of that, Captain." Valda turned away and then, as if at an afterthought, turned back. "And you can come and show me how well you've learned from your mother's instructions. In the meantime, at least your trip wasn't wholly wasted. Trika?" The smirking lieutenant stepped forward. "I trust you will see to it that everyone has a fair turn?"

Trika saluted, and Soleyla saw Rolen staring at her, his eyes wide and frightened. Well, there was no help for it now. It was, after all, what they had planned—the only possible diversion Soleyla had been able to come up with. She returned his gaze, willing him luck and strength, and courage. He

71

bowed his head, slumping, and Soleyla turned away, as if in disgust.

Before she'd gone three paces, when Valda's sharp call stopped her. "Where do you think you're going?"

Soleyla gestured wearily to her filthy uniform. "To the barracks, Commander. I *did* just get back, you know."

"Oh, but Soleyla . . ." Valda's smile glittered with malice, " . . . you really ought to have a chance to see the girls enjoying your present. In fact," she continued, her voice cold, "I insist upon it."

Soleyla hesitated and saw Valda's eyes narrow. If she couldn't get to the gates to open them, couldn't get to the portal to disable it . . . That was to be the signal for Jerril to lead the attack, when he saw the silver shimmer of the portal's field go out. If that didn't happen . . .

If that didn't happen, Rolen would die, and for nothing.

But there was no help for it. Valda cocked her head, gesturing Soleyla toward the ring of women surrounding Rolen. She had to join them, now, before Valda's suspicions grew. Perhaps she could slip away, during the . . .

The *entertainment.*

Soleyla felt her lip curling in distaste but forced herself to stalk back and rejoin the circle.

"Make sure she has a good view, Trika," Valda ordered. "I have things to attend to."

Damn! Soleyla had counted on Valda being distracted by Rolen. He was just the sort the commander liked, big and burly. Soleyla suspected the diminutive woman took a certain perverse pleasure in having such men as slaves. Helplessly, she watched Valda stride to the command center, feeling Trika's gaze on her.

"Want to go first, *Captain* Devarian?"

Gritting her jaw, Soleyla turned back. Some sixty Guardians now ringed Rolen, hemming him in. He crouched in the center, his gaze fixed on her, terrified, pleading. The guards on the wall remained at their posts, but their attention was directed inward, at the scene below them, rather than watching the surrounding hills.

That, at least, was as she'd hoped.

Scanning the faces surrounding Rolen, Soleyla saw a few she recognized. Liatra, her second in command on Termigan IV. Marda, who had been her navigator on that mission. Paula and Perdita, the Betelgeusian twins. Women who knew her intimately enough to read the tension in her stance, the watchfulness of her gaze. Women who had followed her lead once in defiance of the League's commands — and might again. All four of them shipped here, Soleyla was certain, for the same reason she had been, as punishment for that disobedience.

Four. Four Guardians, out of more than sixty. Soleyla found herself hoping fervently that, when the battle started, she wouldn't have to kill them.

In the distance, a low roll of thunder muttered across the sky. Trika glanced up at the lowering clouds, and Soleyla stepped forward hurriedly. They mustn't be allowed to take Rolen into the barracks — she'd never get him out again if they did. And everything depended on keeping the Guardians in the open, vulnerable to attack, and distracted.

Catching Liatra's eye, Soleyla smiled at Trika. "Thank you, Lieutenant. I think I will."

CHAPTER SEVEN

There was a time when Rolen might have chuckled at such an idea. One man, surrounded by half a hundred women! It sounded like the start of a joke, or the sort of grandiose brag boys liked to pass back and forth. But ever since the night he'd hidden, sweating and afraid for his life, behind a thin cover of mountain scrub above the narrow floor of Tinker's Pass, listening to his men die slowly under the sexual attentions of the Guardians who'd ambushed them, Rolen had known a terror that no man should ever experience. A terror, and a shame.

He'd let them die. Carn, Jelken, Ranell. Hidden, he'd lain, his face knotted in agony as he listened to their screams, their desperate pleading. And he had done nothing. It did no good, in the months that followed, to tell himself there was nothing he *could* have done. There had been sixty of them, against his mere dozen. Eight had been killed out of hand. He, Rolen, had barely escaped.

And he'd had to live, ever since, with the sounds of screams in his ears.

Now, kneeling among these same women, Rolen felt a grim satisfaction. This, and this alone, he thought, could wipe that shame away. By submitting himself to the fate they had suffered, Rolen felt redeemed, as if he were finally where he should have been all along — right beside his men, dying with them.

But oh, he was so afraid.

When Soleyla had walked away, a terror deeper than any he had ever known had seized him, turning the wall of faces around him to a blur. He'd wanted to cower, to grovel, begging for his life. Only the thought of his people kept him upright on his knees — Maris, young Betren, Jerril and the others hidden by now along the ridge just above the compound, the women, elders, and children in the camp on the northern plain, the camp these Guardians now knew the location of . . .

Rolen did not grovel. But the fear stayed with him.

Then Valda ordered Soleyla back to the others, and Rolen felt a wave of selfish relief so strong it made him dizzy. But underneath it, a new fear blossomed — what if she couldn't get to the portals?

Rolen still only half believed Soleyla's claim that the portals could transport people instantly from planet to planet. He'd watched the League's scout ship land, disgorging its load of Guardians in full military gear, three months before. But now, looking at the plasteel walls rising around him, Rolen realized they must have been brought, prefabricated, from another planet — and there was only one way they could have been transported so quickly.

If Soleyla couldn't deactivate the portal, his men would be walking into a deathtrap.

Soleyla casually stripped off her muddy clothes, seeming completely unembarrassed by the circle of watching women, and handed them and her sword to two Guardians who looked so alike they had to be twins.

At the sight of the leering, predatory faces surrounding him, Rolen felt the first stirrings of real panic. How was he supposed to get an erection, with so much at stake? All he could think of were the screams of his men, the ones who had died already and the ones who were yet to die . . . unless Soleyla's plan worked.

And that plan, along with the lives of all his people, depended on him.

He closed his eyes, willing himself to arousal, struggling to feel something, *anything*, beyond the churning dread in his gut. He couldn't do it. Those hungry, watching eyes, circling him like a pack of grinning wolves . . . Gods above!

Soleyla's eyes burned into his, dark with warning. Bending over him, she loosened the rope, slipping the noose from around his neck. Then she kicked him, roughly, sending him tumbling into the dirt. He scrabbled forward, hearing the coarse cheers of the watching Guardians, a blank white panic coating his sight. Had she played him, all along? Had it all been a trap, a ruse, to lure him here and leave his people leaderless?

She leapt onto his back, knocking him sprawling. Her fist closed in his hair, yanked his head up. Grinning evilly, she bent close, hissed in his ear. But her words were hardly the threats the watchers would assume from her expression. "Remember, try not to come. There are some who will help us. Be strong. Now, struggle!" She shoved his face forward, grinding it into the mud.

Rolen felt rage surge along his limbs and welcomed it. Anything to drown out that sickly terror. Thrashing, he rolled over, breaking free of her grasp, and heard the laughter around him redouble as he kicked out with his feet, cracking Soleyla across the chin.

Trika hooted. "You've got a live one there, Captain!"

Her face black with fury, Soleyla rose, pointed to two women. "You, and you. Hold him!"

Rolen scrabbled frantically at the rope around his wrists, finally freeing them—too late. The two stepped forward and grabbed his arms, yanking them half out of their sockets as they wrenched him to the ground, pinning him there. Rolen arched against their grasp, not playacting now. Flailing in their grip, he felt a hideous certainty flow through him. Strong as he was, he couldn't break their hold.

Slowly, Soleyla approached, her face, a face he'd come to

know so well, twisted into a sneering mask. "Seems this one doesn't know his place. Shall I teach him, soldiers?" she cried, turning to the Guardians, smiling as they cheered her on — playing, Rolen suddenly recognized, to the crowd. He fell still beneath the hands pinioning him, his chest heaving, waiting.

Her lips curled in a rictus smile, Soleyla approached, stood over him a moment, glaring down. The two women holding him, Rolen noted, were looking up at her, as if for instructions. She squatted beside him, reached for his breechclout. "Now. Let's see what we have, shall we?"

With one sharp tug, she ripped it off him. The Guardians roared their approval. Holding it aloft, she spun, threw it into their midst. A brief tussle ensued. Soleyla's sneer widened, watching it, and Rolen could see the disgust flickering in her eyes. Then she turned back, grabbed his legs, forced them apart. Kneeling between them, she shoved them over her muscular shoulders, dragged his hips to her, raising his ass level with her waist. She leaned forward, her full, gorgeous breasts rubbing across his stomach, and whispered, "Remember this?"

The two women holding him glanced at each other in surprise, but Rolen hardly noticed. He *did* remember. It had been the night before they'd fought in the tent, the night before Soleyla had told him what plan she'd concocted for distracting the Guardians. Tense, driven, sweaty from ten hours spent training his men, she'd been brutal that night, bending him into contortions he'd never so much as imagined, savaging his ass with every implement she could find.

She'd held him, just like this, her erect nipples dragging against his pecs as she'd fucked him, plunging a candle deep in his ass, making Kantou kneel over his face, and watching, her eyes gleaming avidly, as Kantou fucked his mouth.

Gods, yes. He remembered.

Soleyla moved back, revealing his erection, and the

Guardians cheered, their voices more hoarse now, ragged with arousal. Rolen felt them, their watchful expectancy surrounding him like a thick, cloying wave. His cock pulsed, and he didn't fight as she stretched him out, exposing him fully to all those hungry eyes.

There was a weight to their gazes, a heat. He could feel them on his skin, licking his sides, the curve of his ribcage, flicking over his dark, erect nipples and the column of his neck. His cock strained into the air as if displaying itself, eager for their attention, and Rolen felt a shift inside him, as if some part of himself, the part that willed and planned and decided, had fled, leaving only this strange, shameless beast who reveled in their fascination, aroused by their arousal.

Soleyla leaned back on her heels, watching him, a slow lazy smile playing about her lips. Rolen writhed in the dirt before her, enticing her. His hips thrust upward, demonstrating how he would fuck her, and he let his tongue caress his lips in invitation. From the surrounding circle, he heard a deep, excited sigh.

"Perhaps he does know his place, after all. Liatra, turn him loose."

The woman on his left released his wrist, and immediately he raised his hand, running it over the fabric of her shirt, caressing her small, taut breast. Liatra leaned into his touch, enjoying the attention, and looked questioningly at Soleyla.

Rolen hardly noticed. Later, he might say he was only playing a role, merely trying to survive the hideous encounter, but the truth of his arousal pulsed, rigid, against his belly. He *wanted* them to want him, wanted to make them so horny they could think of nothing but fucking him. He wanted to make them come, over and over, coating him in their juices. When Soleyla straddled his shoulders, Rolen reached out eagerly with his tongue, straining his neck upward to taste her. His left hand slid beneath Liatra's shirt to find her nipple while his right caressed the smooth, firm thighs of the third woman.

Soleyla sighed above him, grabbing the other two as if for support as he lapped at her clit. Bending her head, keeping her gaze fixed on his darting tongue, she spoke, low and intent, to the others. "Try to keep him alive. The mood he's in now, he'll be dead within an hour."

"Soleyla . . ." whispered the one on his right.

"Trust me, Marda. Trust me or kill me. They're the only choices you've got."

The words were meaningless to Rolen. He writhed, serpentine, beneath them, darting his tongue deep in Soleyla's cleft, tweaking Liatra's nipple until she groaned with pleasure, bringing their attention back where it belonged — to him. Rolling his eyes, he could see the others beyond them, their faces thick with lust. Most had already shed their clothes. Some caressed each other, or themselves, as they watched him. *Him.* He was the center of it all, the axis on which they spun. He wanted them, all of them, wanted their tits smashed up against him, their clits under his greedy tongue, their slits leaking around his plunging fingers . . .

The sly-faced one with the sneering voice was straddling him now, poising herself above his jutting erection. Trika? Names were meaningless. He thrust his hips upward, spearing her on his cock, and felt her writhe in erotic abandon. Yes. Yes. He would reduce her to nothing, to a moaning, gasping wreck. Rolen smiled as he felt her shudder, pistoned himself up into her again. His right hand worked frantically at the snaps beneath his fingers, freed them, plunged down and in, feeling curly, silken hair, and then a rush of moisture as his fingers burrowed between hot, damp folds.

Soleyla moved above him, and he whimpered as her warmth was withdrawn. Something brushed his cheek and he turned blindly, nuzzling at a full, round breast, sucking the swollen nipple deep into his mouth. Hands moved between his legs, seeking his balls, playing over them, teasing their hardness. Moans and whispers surrounded him, a host of small individual cries that melded into the hoarse panting of one great beast, one magnificent aroused monster he would tease and taunt and fuck until it came, drowning him in its ecstasy, obliterating him.

Yes.

His balls contracted, hot and aching, as the one riding his cock shuddered, her sex gripping his shaft like a vise as she screamed. He thrust, again and again, feeling her passage pulsate around him as another hand probed his sphincter. He was so close to the edge, so close, he could feel his ejaculation rising like a tidal wave inside him, curling, peaking, almost ready to break . . .

A hand slid away from his asshole, gripped the delicate skin between his sphincter and his balls, and pinched *hard*. The pain was sudden, knife-like, and Rolen shrieked, the noise muffled against the tits smashed against his face. The sensual, shameless creature which had overtaken his mind, reveling in their attention, slid away, and Rolen was himself again, aware of where and who he was.

He stiffened in horror. He had come so close, so close to . . . Glancing down, he saw the one Soleyla had beckoned to, Liatra, kneeling between his legs. She winked at him over Trika's heaving shoulder.

Rolen shuddered. How many times could any man orgasm before, spent, he became useless to these women? The sudden return of reality jolted him, and for a moment he was terrified he'd lose his erection. Trika's face, leering down at him, was brutal in its lust—but her slit was slick and tight as a virgin's, and all Rolen had to do was turn his head to find again the nipple he'd been sucking. There was stimulation enough here to keep ten men aroused.

"Going somewhere, Captain?" Trika's voice, brittle with spite, jabbed like a stiletto through the atmosphere of sybaritic excitement, and Rolen looked up. The Guardians paused, their attention momentarily diverted from Rolen, and Soleyla, who had been attempting to slide from their midst unnoticed, froze.

"To the barracks," she replied coldly. "I'm finished—you can have him."

"How generous." Trika smiled. "But the rest of us have only just started." She sat back on Rolen's cock, watching Soleyla through lazy, slitted eyes. Rage seared through him at Trika's greedy, sneering expression, but his groin still burned with agonized need. "Valda would hate for you to miss anything, I know."

Plunging herself down one last time on his aching shaft, the lieutenant rose, gesturing another eager Guardian to take her place. "Save me some," she added to the blonde who lowered herself over him, her breasts bouncing lightly as she slid Rolen's cock into her furnace-like sex. Rolen felt a renewed pulse of desire in his balls, and closed his eyes, thinking of ice, of goat shit, anything to distract him from the scorching, velvety grip of the blonde's slick passage.

When he opened them again, Trika had already pulled on her uniform, and was now ostentatiously strapping her sword belt around her waist. Soleyla hadn't moved. Her sword, Rolen saw, was still in the hands of one of the twins, and Soleyla made no move to reach for it.

She couldn't, he realized, without sparking off a sword fight which would ruin any chance they still had. Trika grinned up at her, almost daring her to argue.

Instead, Soleyla nodded curtly. "As you like," she said, folding her arms across her chest and turning a stony gaze back to the center of the circle. As if that were a signal, the Guardians swarmed around him, their hands stroking his chest, his flanks. One cupped the blonde's breasts as she rode him, fondling them before his eyes. Marda, still kneeling by his shoulders, saw the desperate plea in his gaze and shifted herself over him, blocking the sight of those two perfect breasts being squeezed and stroked. Gratefully, he closed his lips around her clit, sucking it, and felt Marda shiver in wholly unfeigned delight.

Grimly, ignoring the fire that roared through his groin, Rolen set himself to the task of making them come, as many of them as he could, while denying himself, for as long as possible, the release his body craved.

CHAPTER EIGHT

Through all this, Kantou had stood, a lean, pale shadow, near the gates, silent and unmoving. Guardians moved past him, noticing him no more than they would a dog. Glancing at the command center, he'd seen Valda watching through the large upper window, but for now she had disappeared.

Soleyla had been moving toward him, working her way surreptitiously through the intent, distracted ring of women, but at Trika's call she had stopped. Now she stood, her jaw clenched as she watched the Guardians descend on Rolen, the ring around him growing smaller, tighter, as each fought for her turn at him.

Kantou's gut churned. If Soleyla couldn't get free without causing a ruckus ... Above him, the Guardians still on the wall had abandoned their posts, gathering above the gate as they watched, their eyes gleaming avidly even in the dull, murky light. Thunder pealed across the sky, but not one of them so much as lifted her head from the titillating gang-bang going on below. Kantou swallowed and edged backward until the wall hid them from his sight.

Rapidly now, he turned, scanning the wall. The control box was twenty feet to his left, inside a small booth. The Guardian posted there was lounging against the door, her gaze fixed on the heaving bodies surrounding Rolen. Her hand worked inside her pants as she masturbated.

Kantou swallowed. If he was caught, there would be no mercy. And no second chance—all of them would die. But Soleyla was trapped under Trika's watchful gaze. There was no one else.

Slowly, silently, he slid along the wall toward the control booth.

Soleyla stood, her arms folded, her face a dispassionate mask. Inside, though, she seethed with frustration. How long could Rolen hold himself back under that hungry, licking, moaning mass of women? Not even Kantou, with his iron control, could survive it.

Kantou, she thought suddenly, panicked. He'd been just there, near the wall. Now he was gone. Her eyes darted, searching the gloom. Damn this weather! Thunder roared overhead, sending a jolt through her, raising her need to move, to act, to a fever pitch. Time pressed in on her, she could feel it, trickling, trickling . . .

Where was Kantou?

"Looking for something, Devarian?"

Soleyla let her lip curl in disdain. "Something more interesting than this." She gestured disgustedly and turned away. Steel whispered on steel as Trika drew her blade, stopping her before she'd taken two steps.

"The commander gave you an order, Devarian."

"Fine. She can court-martial me, for all I care." Soleyla's limbs quivered with tension. The static electricity in the air seared along her blood. Somewhere, on the ridge above the compound, the Antoreans crouched, nervously waiting. Behind the ring of writhing women, Soleyla heard Rolen groan, his voice thick with agony.

There was no more time. Where in *hell* was Kantou?

Holding his breath, Kantou squeezed himself into the corner between the control booth and the wall. Not three feet in front of him, the Guardian panted, her fingers mashing her clit. Her eyes were half-closed, her head tilted back. There'd be no better chance.

Lunging forward, Kantou locked his fists together, raised them in the air and brought them smashing down on the back of the Guardian's neck. There was an awful, sickening snap, and the woman tumbled to the ground. Kantou's stomach heaved, but there was no time. Glancing about rapidly, he dragged her body into the control booth, shoved it against one wall, and turned to the panel.

All his life, he'd had a gift for seeing how things worked. In the child-house on Marbul, the technicians who serviced the machinery had liked him, ruffling his hair as they allowed him to hold their wrenches and circuit-testers, just as if he'd been a tech-slave, he'd thought excitedly. He'd watched eagerly, *knowing* without being told why they'd attached that wire there, replaced this servo-gear here. When he'd adjusted Soleyla's tracker, it had been without permission, and he'd trembled the entire time with fear at his audacity. But his desire, his craving to peer into its intricate depths, to retune the instrument to its greatest capacity, had been irresistible.

Now his keen gray eyes flicked over the control panel. It was simple enough, he saw, and felt almost disappointed. Locking mechanism here, the lever that opened and closed the gates there. Quickly, he flicked the lock off, debated, glanced out the door at the roiling sky, and reached for the lever.

The gates had opened noiselessly, obviously powered by the great generators on the far side of the command center. Even unlocked, it was entirely possible that without that power they would remain immobile however the Antoreans tugged and yanked. Wincing at the risk he was taking, Kantou pulled the lever gingerly, peering through the gloom at the barely visible gates.

They cracked open, one foot, two feet, three . . . The guards above them appeared oblivious. Hastily, Kantou shoved the lever back to neutral, and slid out of the booth.

There! Just a flicker of movement, in the shadow of the wall. He was coming outof the control booth. And that meant . . .

Soleyla glanced rapidly, hoping Trika wouldn't notice the direction of her gaze. Yes. He'd done it. Her brave, clever, beautiful Kantou! He stared at her, his eyes flicking toward the portal. Soleyla nodded, a minute, unnoticeable jerk of her chin. She'd have to trust him. There was no chance at all she'd be able to get to the portals herself.

Soleyla glanced back as Trika growled behind her, "I suggest you follow your orders, Captain."

Grinning at the dark-haired lieutenant, Soleyla turned to face her squarely. "And I suggest you *make* me, you cunt-licking grunt."

Trika shrieked in rage, raising her sword. "Captain!" Perdita shouted and flung Soleyla's sword as she ducked under Trika's first stroke. Catching it by the hilt, she rolled, coming up to block Trika's second, furious swing.

Her only hope now was to keep Trika distracted, to keep the focus on her long enough to give Kantou a chance. The crush around Rolen was thinning as the Guardians, drawn by the fight, abandoned him for this new entertainment. Soleyla strained to catch a glimpse of him, but Trika lunged at her.

She spun, disdainfully slapping the lieutenant's thrust aside. As Trika stumbled, off balance, Soleyla held back the instinctive, lethal blow that had been drilled into her, settling instead for swatting Trika's rump with the flat of her sword. The Guardians laughed and Trika, stung to incoherent fury, wheeled, her blade cutting in a deadly arc before her.

Dancing aside, Soleyla jabbed lightly, pricking Trika's ribs.

The lieutenant screamed like a banshee and grabbed Soleyla's sword, slashing her left hand open to immobilize the blade, while with her right she whirled her sword in a flat sweep at Soleyla's neck.

She was fighting a madwoman, Soleyla realized. Some ugly, jealous creature inside the lieutenant didn't give a damn whether she lived or died, so long as she could kill the beautiful, haughty senator's daughter. Easy enough to wrench her blade from Trika's grasp, laying her palm open to the bones — but in the moment it would take, Trika's sword would find her throat.

All this passed through her mind in a flash — and then Soleyla was diving under the oncoming blade, rolling on the muddy ground to spring back to her feet. The Guardians, she saw, had forgotten Rolen entirely. Only Liatra remained beside him, cradling his unconscious — or dead — body. But now Trika had both swords, and Soleyla was weaponless.

Thunder roared overhead. Trika didn't so much as look up. Flipping Soleyla's blade in the air, she caught it by the grip. Blood sprayed across her face as the pommel slapped into her lacerated palm, but the lieutenant grinned, seeming to feel no pain.

Soleyla backed away, aware of the press of the crowd behind her, limiting her range of motion. Lightning streaked across the sky, and by its sudden, dazzling light she saw Valda storming from the command center.

The Guardians so far had been content to watch, entertained by the animosity between the two officers. But the second Valda gave the order, they would crush her.

Soleyla stared about, desperate, then reeled back as, with a high, almost inaudible shriek, a second bolt of lightning slashed down, stabbing at the thin white spire of the comm tower. It exploded, sending sparks flying, and Soleyla heard the whine of overstressed dynamos spiraling up to an impossible pitch. For a heartbeat, the whole world went black. The silver sheen of the portals flickered, blazed to white, and went out.

With a fierce, exultant shout, Soleyla leapt, landing a punishing kick in Trika's gut. The lieutenant staggered backward, collapsed, and Soleyla's sword flew from her nerveless hand. Seizing it up, Soleyla spun, driving her sword down at Trika's prone form — then froze as an ominous groan filled the air.

Looking up, she saw the shattered, blackened comm tower listing, its supports screeching as, one by one, they snapped. Guardians dove for cover as it fell, smashing one of the barracks. Thunder crashed overhead, and with a hiss like that of a giant snake, the rain descended, furious and unrelenting.

Through its heavy veil, Soleyla made out Valda's short, stocky form, frozen at the wreckage before her. Then, beyond Valda, she saw Kantou, halfway across the compound, racing for the utility portal. But the portal was already out!

No. Soleyla's stomach lurched as, with a grinding crunch, the generators churned back to life. The portals, both the massive utility portal and the smaller personnel one, near the command center, came back online, their silver sheen reflecting off the pelting rain. Soleyla's heart sank as she heard, over the clamor and the roar of flames from the barracks, a Guardian high on the wall, shouting into her headset.

Jerril had attacked.

And the portal wasn't down.

Soleyla whirled. The Antoreans were pouring in a mass through the gates, heaving them wide, slashing into the dazed, disorganized Guardians. Valda stared, glaring murderously across the compound, then wheeled and ran for the command center. Soleyla pelted after her. If the commander got more troops through that portal . . . Suddenly she was flung headlong into the mud. Her sword flew from nerveless fingers as a booted foot smashed down between her shoulder blades, sending a flare of agony down her spine.

"I asked this before, I'll ask it again," Trika panted, bending low over her. "Going somewhere, Captain?"

The slap of cold rain slowly roused Rolen. Retching, he rolled to his knees, a watery weakness trembling along his limbs. Someone was behind him, touching him . . . Rolen flinched, felt his overstrained muscles give way, and collapsed, flailing helplessly in the soupy mud.

"Rolen!" A voice, in his ear, shouting above the roar of the rain. A woman's voice.

"Soleyla?" The word was a croak. He opened his eyes a slit, made out a pair of clear hazel eyes, soft with concern.

"I'm Liatra. Remember?"

He could remember nothing. The past was a blurred, writhing darkness, the present a roaring, screaming chaos that lacerated his nerves. Something exploded, sending sputtering sparks streaking through the darkness, and Rolen cowered in the mud, hiding his eyes.

The portal loomed before Kantou, the air within its frame seeming to quiver with light. It pulsed, building in intensity, and Kantou knew with that instinctive comprehension that it was in use.

Something was coming through.

Like a giant picture frame, the portal stretched across the muddy ground, fifteen meters across and five high, a white plasteel bracket without break or joint, and no controls that he could see. *No,* he realized, appalled, *of course not. They're in the command center. Not here. Not . . .*

His mind raced. The controls might not be accessible, but it still needed a power source, either its own power-pack, or . . .

The generator. The portal had gone out when the generator died.

The swirling, flickering illumination inside the portal increased, building to a flat white glare. The generators were on the far side, behind the command center. So, too, would be the cables. Sprinting, he dashed past the front of the portal, his outline stark against its glowing light. Well, there was no help for it — if he was seen, he was seen.

Something seemed to waver inside that glow, a suggestion of shadow, of movement. Lunging, he dove the final four meters, cleared the frame, scrabbled blindly in the thick mud, searching . . .

There!

The cable was thicker than his thigh, coated in heavy rubber. It ran to a plate, bolted securely to the frame, four feet off the ground. Kantou stared at it in dismay. It was hopeless. He had nothing, not a wrench, not even a knife. Electricity hummed through the cable at his feet, and he was powerless to stop it.

A shout rose behind him and Kantou whirled, crouching. He had been seen. Two grim-faced Guardians were pounding toward him. Behind them he could see Valda, screaming an order. He didn't need to hear her words to know they meant his death — the drawn swords gleaming in the Guardians' fists told him clearly enough.

The clash of steel on steel surrounded Soleyla, and she knew the Antorean men were attacking the disorganized Guardians. But their advantage was rapidly fading as, by twos and threes, the League soldiers responded to Valda's stentorian shouts and broke away from the onslaught to fall back and regroup.

She thrashed desperately. Her left leg didn't seem to be

responding. Trika's boot ground into her back, sending waves of agony down her spine. Was it shattered? She couldn't tell. A razor-sharp blade touched the side of her neck, and Soleyla ceased her struggles.

"Kill me, bitch," she growled, tasting gritty mud on her tongue. "Go ahead and kill me, if you dare."

"Oh, I dare, Guardian." Soleyla felt the blade removed as Trika hefted her sword for the killing blow. She raised her head, hoping for one last glimpse of Kantou, but there was nothing but the blur of rain, the flash of lightning . . .

She had failed. And now she, and everyone she loved, would die.

She screamed, hoping he would hear her, wherever he was, hoping he would know, in his remaining moments, that he had been the final thing in her thoughts.

"*Kantou!*"

Trika grinned, hearing the despair in Soleyla's voice. At last the haughty bitch knew her place in the world. She and her fancy boy, and that black-haired ox she'd found. Whatever the old tune might say, it appeared money *did* buy love — and Trika would have plenty of it, now. Valda would reward her well for this traitor's death.

She raised her sword, savoring the moment . . . and staggered forward as someone shoved her from behind. A furious bellowing filled her ears and she turned, bringing her sword up.

No. Impossible. He should be dead, *dead!* No man could survive what had been done to him. They didn't have the strength, the stamina. She'd *seen* him, a useless hulk sprawled on the ground, empty and limp as a drained wineskin.

Snarling, he crouched over Soleyla, glaring up at her — but Trika noticed the way his arms trembled, the way his legs quivered with strain, and smiled. He wasn't dead, but he would be. Soon. Men were so weak. He barely had the strength to keep himself from collapsing on top of the woman he shielded.

At that, a bitter envy flared through Trika. No one had ever shielded *her*. No one had ever taken *her* to Porto, bought *her* a fancy pleasure slave. No one had used their influence to gain her a commission; she'd had to earn it, every grinding, exhausting, ass-kissing step of the way. No one had ever—Trika felt bile burn in the pit of her stomach, felt rage race like wildfire along her limbs as Rolen glared up at her, defending the daughter of the woman who'd ordered his enslavement— loved *her*.

Screeching like an enraged cat, she plunged her sword at Rolen, knowing he was too weak to stand, much less fight her. *Men,* she sneered silently, *just don't have the stamina.*

As Rolen rolled to one side, seizing Soleyla's sword and thrusting it up through her belly, Trika discovered just how little she knew about men.

"Kantou!"

At Soleyla's scream, Kantou's head jerked up. Looking past the Guardians racing toward him, he saw the League soldiers falling back, regrouping. Rolen, standing over Soleyla with her sword in his hands, staggered and collapsed heavily to one knee. Jerril and the Antoreans swept past them, forming a thick protective line between them and the command center.

There were some thirty Guardians remaining, grouped in a tight knot before the command center's main entrance, shielding it against the Antorean men. Valda had disappeared, inside, Kantou assumed.

Anguish twisted through him as he realized how close they'd come, how heartbreakingly close. Then the two soldiers rushed him, and he stumbled back, tripping over the portal's power cable.

An almost inaudible whine pierced his skull, and the portal frame seemed to pulse with light. The support troops were coming through.

It was all over.

He rolled as a blade sliced down at him, wondering even as he did so why he was bothering. It bit into the thick rubber casing of the cable just where his neck had been not a second before. As the second sword flashed down, even as he dove aside, he saw again in his mind's eye that first blade arcing down, slashing deep into the cable — and Kantou knew he had one last, slim, impossible chance.

Crouched beside Soleyla, shaking with exhaustion, Rolen nodded toward the men holding the few remaining soldiers at bay.

"Damned if we didn't do it, Guardian." He gave her a wide, tremulous grin.

"No." Soleyla pushed herself up on her arms, dragging her right leg awkwardly behind her. "We didn't." Her gaze, black and burning, was turned past him, ignoring the face-off before the control center.

Rolen turned — and froze, feeling victory slip like sodden ashes into despair. Between the gleaming posts of the portal, a wall of fresh troops, thirty across, were pushing through what looked like a veil of light, ripping it. Behind them, dimly, he could see more ranks massed, waiting to come through.

And there was nothing they could do, not any of them, to stop it. Rolen groaned and hid his face in despair.

Kantou lunged again, desperately, just ahead of the two

blades. He had to do this right, had to get the angle, the momentum . . . Pistoning to his feet, he turned to run — and stumbled in the mud. He threw his arms out hopelessly, but the ground rushed up at him. The cable snapped his head back, smashed brutally against his windpipe as he fell, his neck stretched across the cable, a perfect, irresistible target. Stunned, he lay, hearing the two Guardians pounce, their swords raised for the blow — and threw himself aside just as their blades whistled down.

League-forged steel, tempered to a scalpel-like sharpness, sheared through the thick rubber as if it were cloth. Sparks flew as metal bit into wire, and Kantou, panting, one cheek pressed to the ground, watched the Guardians arch, their skin and hair and nostrils smoking, as raw electricity flowed through their swords and into their bodies.

Behind him, the portal's field flickered spastically, and he heard a brief, truncated shriek as the shock wave seared the support troops, cleaving them as neatly as a laser. The whine of the generators spiraled to an impossibly high pitch, throbbed once, and dropped back down as an emergency switch tripped, cutting power to the cable. The dead Guardians fell, their bodies burnt and twisted. Sickened, Kantou gagged, then staggered to his feet. Ahead, he could see the field of the smaller portal glowing. The thick air smelled of ozone, and charred flesh. It scraped at his throat as he ran, pausing only to bend and snatch a sword from the hand of a fallen Antorean.

There was a metallic thud behind him, and a shriek of rage. Kantou caught a glimpse of Valda, her face contorted in fury, slamming through the side door of the command center and pounding after him.

"Kantou!"

Soleyla heaved herself up, fell back as her right leg collapsed under her. The tendons in her neck stood out as she dragged herself back to her feet, lurched into a run, overriding the agony that stabbed up her leg at every stride. "Kantou!" she screamed again.

Behind her, she could hear Rolen staggering, trying to follow. He shouted instead, and from the corner of her eye Soleyla saw a handful of men peel away from the group surrounding the defeated Guardians. They dashed after her through the pelting rain, but it was too far, the gap was too wide . . . Reaching for every last, desperate ounce of her formidable will, Soleyla sprinted, overriding crushed nerves and screaming tendons, and gained a yard on Valda, two . . .

Kantou was hacking desperately at the power cable. Valda threw herself at him. Behind them, the portal blazed, and Soleyla lunged forward, shrieking like an enraged hawk. Valda didn't even glance at her as she seized Kantou, yanking him away from the cable. Grabbing his hair, she spun him to face Soleyla, drew his head back and laid her sword across his throat.

Soleyla staggered to a stop, gasping, pleading mutely with the gray-haired woman. Behind her, she heard the men rushing up, and frantically waved them back. Time seemed to stop, freezing them in an eternal tableau. In it, Soleyla could note every treasured, familiar curve of Kantou's face; the frightened, yearning gaze of his clear gray eyes; the way his beautiful, ash-brown hair fell, gleaming, over his shoulders; the throb of the artery in his long, graceful neck, just underneath the cruelly keen edge of Valda's blade.

Contemptuously, Valda watched Soleyla's face go deathly pale, and sneered with disdain. "Is this what you did it for? A *slave*?" Her voice was incredulous.

Soleyla panted, unable to answer.

Valda curved her lips into a smile as sharp as a knife.

"Congratulations, Soleyla. You've succeeded. Antoros is yours . . . for what it's worth." Her eyes raked the bloody, mud-spattered men holding the remaining Guardians at sword point. "I hope you enjoy the taste of your victory."

She moved suddenly, and Soleyla watched in horror as, with a contemptuous shove, Valda propelled Kantou into the blazing field of the portal. Whirling, the commander raised her sword, and with one murderous sweep severed the cable. Her body jerked, seared by the power pulsing through her sword, and immediately the portal went black.

"*No!*"

Soleyla lunged forward as Valda fell. Rain poured down, thudding around her as the generators whined once and died. Screaming, Soleyla drove her sword, uselessly, through Valda's lifeless chest, again and again and again. But it was too late.

Kantou was gone.

Don't Miss the Exciting Conclusion In:

Devarian Revolution.

Available May 5th, 2023 at Extasy Books and many other booksellers.

Driven by her grief and fury at the loss of Kantou, Soleyla Devarian leads her forces to victory against the Nine-Star League. Planet after planet falls to Soleyla's revolution, aided by the slaves who rally to her cause. Now the only hurdle remaining is the conquest of Argulus, the capitol planet of the

Nine-Star League, ruled by Soleyla's mother.

In a deadly face-off between mother and daughter, Soleyla finally learns the shocking fate of Danel, her first pleasure slave—and discovers that Rachel Devarian holds Kantou's fate in her cold grasp as well. Can Soleyla find a way to save her beloved Kantou, or must she sacrifice the man she loves to save the galaxy from her mother's tyranny?

ABOUT THE AUTHOR

Sierra Dafoe has a thing for hot romantic heroes, cool ocean breezes, and — of all things — chickens. The day she figures out how to keep livestock on a sailboat, she's moving to the Caribbean.

An award-winning author who garnered three CAPA nominations in her first year of publishing, Sierra has gone on to receive numerous awards and recommended reads for her work. Her home on the web is sierradafoe.com, where you can find excerpts, sneak peeks, and all her latest news. Sign up for her newsletter for a special monthly contest!

www.ingramcontent.com/pod-product-compliance
Lightning Source LLC
Chambersburg PA
CBHW071128130626
46555CB00016B/1190